BLOOD & Flowers

ALSO BY PENNY BLUBAUGH
Serendipity Market

PENNY BLUBAUGH

BLOOD & Flowers

HARPER TEEN

An Imprint of HarperCollins*Publishers*

HarperTeen is an imprint of HarperCollins Publishers.

Blood & Flowers

www.harperteen.com

Library of Congress Cataloging-in-Publication Data
Blubaugh, Penny.
  Blood & flowers / Penny Blubaugh. — 1st ed.
    p. cm.
  Summary: When the Outlaw Puppet Troupe is accused of various
crimes by a vengeful critic, the members escape to the faerie world to
avoid being incarcerated.
  ISBN 978-0-06-172862-4
  [1. Fairies—Fiction. 2. Supernatural—Fiction. 3. Puppet theater—
Fiction. 4. Interpersonal relations—Fiction.] I. Title.
PZ7.B6245Bl 2011   2010004603
[Fic]—dc22   CIP
                                                                     AC

Typography by Sarah Hoy
11 12 13 14 15   CG/RRDB   10 9 8 7 6 5 4 3 2 1

First Edition

In memory of Sharon Ball, who always believed this book would happen. I miss you every day.

In memory of Dewis, the best cat ever.

I

"You'll know it when you find it."

"*I*n case you don't know, you use a thin paste of the flour water to stick the flyer down. Put them on boards, telephone poles, newspaper boxes—whatever. The paste dries hard, but it's clear and a bitch to get off."

I demoed the process to Lucia and slapped one of our flyers on the wood covering the broken window of Clem's Furniture Store (furniture long, long gone). Then I handed her the paste tub. "Your turn."

Lucia worked carefully, setting her flyer next to mine. A double whammy. The manicured nails on her scarred hands were perfect, cream with ebony tips. Her hands were graceful, and when they moved, her scars flared in the just-turning-on streetlights. She finished and looked over at me. "Persia? How's that?"

I had to make myself stop watching her and look at the side-by-side flyers. There's something about Lucia that makes me wish I were gay. Maybe it's her quiet sadness just below the surface. If we were more than friends I'd feel like I had a reason to protect her. But we were just Lucia and Persia. "Perfect," I told her.

Our flyers said:

OUTLAW PUPPET TROUPE

presents
The Bastard and the Beauty
A play of love, dislike, and anticorruption
Place: You'll know it when you find it
Date: Now and then
Time: Eight o'clock, usually. At night.
But things can always change.

Lucia examined her pasted flyer and tapped it with one of those gorgeous nails. "It doesn't say anything about the magic that's in this show."

"You know we never like to draw too much attention to that."

"I know." Lucia nodded. "The anti-fey feelings all around town. The idea that magic is bad. But people should know that this is good magic."

I made a little hissing noise; then I said, "If we're going to flout convention and get in trouble about magic, why not just put in the whole soap-bubble theory to tell them how the magic gets here in the first place?"

Lucia looked confused. "I don't know the soap-bubble theory. Is it long? Because this is a small flyer."

I raised my eyebrows. "You mean I've never explained my 'how the fey get into our world' theory to you? Wow. I must be slipping."

"You could tell me while we work," she said.

She actually seemed interested. Not many people did, which always surprised me. I thought it was a brilliant theory. I straightened my shoulders, right there in front of Clem's, and pretended I was giving a speech. "Faerie skims around our world like a soap bubble around a glass. When the bubble of us meets one of the bubbles of them, the membranes collapse

3

and the fey can access our world. This only seems to work one way."

"Not always," Lucia said. She spoke in such a quiet voice I almost missed her comment. Almost, but not quite.

I'd forgotten that Lucia had wished herself into Faerie once, a long time ago. "So I'm wrong?" I asked. I flushed and added, "You probably know all about this, and I probably sound so stupid."

Lucia shook her head. "I don't have any idea about how people go from one side to the other. I don't know how I did it. It just happened, like a sneeze. But your theory makes as much sense as anyone else's."

I blinked three times and said, "You mean I could be right?"

Lucia nodded and I said, "How cool is that? I made it up on my own, you know." I beamed at her.

"It's better than anything I've ever come up with. But back to this." She tapped the flyer one more time. "It might not make people come. We're not telling them about the wonders."

Lucia had a point. I mean, we weren't passing out

a lot of information. But there's a reason and it's right there in the name: Outlaw Puppet Troupe. We're obviously not going for mainstream or even politically correct. Social and political commentary is a big part of every production, and there's never a lack of something to say.

We live in a world with lots of problems. The environment is in trouble, the economy's tumbling, and there's crime on the corners and corruption in the capital. Look back through history and you'll see that these are the kinds of problems that could be problems anywhere, anytime. But here and now, and ever since I can remember, really, the inhabitants of Faerie are blamed for almost everything that goes wrong. Most of that blame starts with our government. I'm not sure why, and I don't remember hearing about it in any history class I ever took. But I know there's antagonism.

I have an antagonism theory, too, to go with my soap-bubble one. It's all about the anti-fey sentiments in our world and where they come from. If I'd given Lucia a speech about that, it would have sounded like this: "When you've got plans for power and domination, you need something besides your own activities to occupy people. One of the best ways to occupy people is to give them a common enemy. A good way to identify an enemy is to point out how different they are. The fey are different—they always have been. Bingo! Adversary right here! Now just throw out some media misinformation and you're on your way. Everyone concentrates on the evilness of the different, and no one has time to pay attention to anything else."

But even though some fey surely are evil, they can't possibly be causing all of the wacky things we deal with on a daily basis. At least I don't think so, but here are samples of the kinds of stories that float around my world.

POINT YOUR FINGER AT THE FEY

Crime? Fey problem. (*Bugle-Express*—Faerie Breaks into Shop—Steals Diamonds!)

Failing Neighborhoods? Fey problem. (*Daily Times*—Faerie Landlord Lets Building Collapse! Also—Faerie Gangs Run Rampant!)

Sick environment? Fey problem. (*You and Me Magazine*—Faeries Blow Poison Dust across Border!)

Drug abuse? Fey problem. (Government Report 2693-6, Paragraph 3—"It has been noted and corroborated that dangerous drinks and drugs have been coming from Faerie on a regular basis. Citizens are warned to be wary." Or, as Senator Reynolds has said, sounding a lot more nervous—"Danger! Faerie Drinks and Dust on the Rise!")

Total eclipse? Fey problem. (Talk Radio WKQS—"Fey stealing life-giving sunshine with magic! Call, starting at midnight, with your comments!")

If I had the urge to call WKQS (which I would never have), I'd say I see no problem with magic, or with the fey. First, magic is in all of our productions. Sometimes that magic is subtle, and sometimes not so much, but it's always there. And, of course, fey Floss is our chief costumer and puppet guru. If Faerie puppet magic and the sly social jibes we always incorporate don't make us outlaws, then I don't know what would.

Lucia looked again at our side-by-side flyers and smoothed one corner. "I still like telling about the magical wonders."

"We'll mention it to Tonio," I said, "for next time."

Lucia grinned, and we moved down the street to a convenient light pole.

Tonio is artistic director for the Outlaws. It still seems strange to me to think that we even have something like an artistic director, but it's as good a title as any. After all, he's artistic in a very flamboyant, very gay way—which he also is. Gay, I mean. And he certainly directs this sloppy, flopping mass we call a troupe.

When I first met Tonio I was fifteen, standing on the corner of Main and Paris, looking tough, or trying to, because Main and Paris is not the neighborhood where you want to look anything but tough. And down the street came this guy, tall and slim, with moves like a drag queen, an ankle-length cape lined with whiskey-shot silver, and a handful of hot pink flyers. He was slapping those flyers up on any open surface, using a twee little paste pot. When he got even with me he stopped, looked me up and down, nodded, and said, "Here."

My first thought was that he was one of the resident pixie dust dealers, just cleaner and much better dressed. So I didn't ask what "Here" meant. I just stepped aside because nobody wants to be seen with a dust dealer.

It's not like people don't know there are dealers. And it's not like those dealers can't find people who use—you can find dust dippers any night, if you're looking. They're the shadows in doorways, careful to stay out of the streetlight circles. It's just that nobody wants to be blatantly involved with dust, or its companion, the wild-colored drinks that are as illegal as the dust and that slide along the same pathways.

This guy shoved his papers at me anyway. "I need a

flyer person. It's too much of a pain to do it all alone. You look like you can handle it. Slap 'em up anywhere and I'll glue 'em down."

And just like that, I was part of the Outlaws. Because, you see, I did take the flyers, and I didn't even ask why. There's something very persuasive about Tonio, even when he's not trying.

There's also something otherworldly about him. For the longest time I thought he might be part fey, but no. He's just Tonio. He may be entirely mortal but he can see you and understand all about your anima. Snap! Because why else would he look twice at a fifteen-year-old girl with a penchant for dropping out of school, a mile-wide love of Shakespeare, and drugged-out, fey-bashing parents who walked through life in a fog that never involved their daughter? I scanned the flyers that day as I held them against the walls and poles. "Puppets?" I'd asked, and okay, I'd sneered.

Tonio, without really looking at me, had said, "Yes, darling. Puppets."

I'd wiggled my fingers at him, making little

air-shadow rabbits.

And he'd laughed. Tonio has a great laugh. It's deep and brassy, and it sounds like happy bassoons. When he was done laughing he shook his head, still grinning. "You looked like one of the open-minded ones." And then he had looked at me, really looked, and I'd been caught by his eyes, deep green, rimmed with gold, and I'd stopped moving, stopped breathing, it seemed.

After a couple of minutes, or maybe a few days, he'd said, "Oh, good. I was right after all. You just need some training." He'd swept off down the street, and without thinking at all, I'd followed. Welcome to the Outlaws. Finding them was like coming home to the place I'd been looking for forever.

That was three years ago. Last year I left my parents for good and became a full-time Outlaw. The good things stick.

The Outlaws don't do shadow puppets, and they never do felt replicas of Little Bo Peep. They don't do fuzzy Santas in fleece suits and I've never once, in three years, seen anyone work with a dragon with silk and Mylar flames waving in its mouth. Although I thought this would have been dax beyond belief. Tonio says this is why I'm not artistic director. Floss just sneers and says no way is she using her fine and excellent stitches to make something as painful as a dragon with phony flames, and besides, dragons hardly ever do that, anyway, and she should know.

"Persia," Lucia said, "I gave my last good flyer to the people in Breadbox. The ones I have left all have crumbles, the paste is gone, and it's getting too dark to see. We're close to that strip where the pink and purple drinks are supposed to come out after dark, and that's always scary. Sometimes there's pixie dust, too, or at least that's what people say. We should go home. And anyway, isn't someone making pizza?"

"If by someone you mean me, no."

"You have no idea how thankful that makes me. I was hoping for something edible."

Normally when I'm dissed I sling back. But Lucia? I let her get away with murder.

REASONS FOR LETTING LUCIA GET
AWAY WITH MURDER

She's fragile and delicate.

She's still working over a very creepy childhood. (See previous bit about scars.)

She's smarter than me and will always come out on top.

She's my friend, and in that role she is allowed special dispensation.

She's right about the strip. Pink and red drinks, blue and purple. Like the pixie dust, they're gifts from somewhere (and here I'd have to admit that most of this stuff does seem Faerie-related) that have been booming lately.

This is her first time hanging flyers, which can certainly be an irritating way to spend an afternoon, especially when it's getting dark and starting to rain.

So I only said, "Be glad Max is cooking then," and we went down into the sub station, catching our heels on the old steps with the scuffed red edges. Lucia had been right about it being time to leave. We passed one person who already looked dusted, even though it was still early in the evening. He was sitting on the steps next to where my left foot came down when I turned a corner, but all he did was hold out his hand, look hopeful, and say, "Change? Any spare change?" in a beautiful baritone voice. I shook my head and walked on by feeling sorry for him, feeling glad for myself. It would have been so easy to have landed in the same place.

Once we'd paid our fare, we muscled our way through the wood-barred turnstiles and out onto the platform. Within ten minutes we'd caught the Conroy Street sub and we were headed for home.

II

"Mushrooms? Waxed thread?"

ome. I call the Outlaws home, which is actually funny in an ironic sort of way because they don't have one. Not if home is understood to mean a permanent space, or a stage that you can always come back to. We perform wherever—we're all over the city. Part of that is for safety because, political outlaws that we are, we're not always popular with authority figures. Part of that is because we work with Floss. That fey magic problem always looms large, with dangerous connotations. We all know it's Floss's magic, of course, and we know she'd never do anything during a show except use that magic to make things spectacular. But you can't always count on people to make the right distinctions. For every show, we walk a thin line, somewhere between walloping them with magic and letting the script and the puppets do their work.

Mostly, though, we move around the city because we want everyone to get a chance to see us, money and social status never being a factor. All that movement is worth it, too, because it allows us to do what we want, say what we want, and comment on whatever pops into our heads. I believe that we have unparalleled freedom, and to me that's more dax than anything.

We use Tonio and Max's apartment to house paraphernalia, mostly because Tonio is Tonio, after all, and almost but not quite mostly because Max scored a huge apartment when his parents tried to buy him off so he'd quit being gay. He stayed gay, especially after he met Tonio, but he kept the apartment out of "spite, or maybe pure, cussed meanness," as he likes to say.

It's good they have this place, Max and Tonio, because Lucia's got pretty much nothing, Nicholas still lives in the dorms, Floss sometimes blinks in and out to see unnamed inhabitants of Faerie, and I, of course, escaped from my parents' drug-haven house. Max and Tonio provided for me, just as they provided for Floss and Lucia, and I'm eternally grateful.

It's also good because Max cooks like a dream, and he always makes enough food for at least a dozen people.

Lucia and I got out at the Ringley stop, turned right off of Conroy, and took Ringley four blocks to Max and Tonio's. Four grubby blocks, with squashy trash underfoot and papery trash flying overhead. Nice people, mostly, just not a lot of cash. Still, every once in a while you catch a dust deal going down, like a relic from another time. Usually by the time you turn to face it straight on, the deal's done and what's left is a shoe heel, or the tail of a coat disappearing around the side of a Dumpster. But you can catch remnants of what just happened hanging in the air. Things feel, for one long second, a little jittery, a bit jumpy. And you realize for that same long second that you're holding your breath.

All of this makes stepping onto the corner of

Barnard, a kind of upscale block in the middle of downscale, feel warm even when it's cold and rainy. Then you might step into Max and Tonio's, and the feeling changes all over again, because stepping into their place is like stepping into a circus.

WHY MAX AND TONIO'S IS LIKE A CIRCUS

The walls are scarlet and gold, maroon and blue, grass green and Day-Glo yellow.

The ceilings are so high that the lights can't get all the way up. I always feel like golden lion tamarins are hiding up there, waiting to swing down on me. Or like there are hidden trapezes.

Everything looks cheerful. And messy clean. And the place smells like good food and sharp wine and wheat paste glue.

Confetti shreds of newspaper dance on the floor with pieces of silk ribbons and fake flower petals—left-overs from puppets and masks.

There's always music. Sometimes classical (that's Max), sometimes sad folk (Tonio), and sometimes gypsy caravan guitar (that's both of them). Nicholas and

I switch things over to singer-songwriter and punk
when we feel like it. Floss sings long complicated
songs about Faerie that I never quite understand.
Lucia quietly appreciates all of it.

When Lucia and I opened the door, Nicholas almost rammed us. "Sorry," he said, his voice light and breathless. "Mushrooms." And he clattered down the stairs, leaving a scent of lemon in the air.

I leaned over the railing to watch him slam out the front door. Nicholas. Preppy law student Nicholas, who loves lighting sets as much as he loves the law, is why I can just look at Lucia and never act. How can the drug droppers' kid be interested in an almost-lawyer? Who knows? The world's a mysterious place.

Lucia and I banged the door closed and I yelled, "We're here," and Tonio yelled back, "How many flyers did you get up?"

Lucia said, "We ran out of paste."

"But it's okay," I said, "because we got pretty much everything blanketed between Paris and Milan."

Floss floated into the dining room and bellowed,

"Waxed thread?" Floss's dandelion hair and almost see-through presence contrast strongly with her dockworker voice. Some people say Floss is scary strong. When they describe her it's as if she's bigger than life, some mythological creature. I don't get that. To me, she's just Floss, sort of ethereal and solid at the same time. Still, Floss is not someone you want to upset.

"Oops," said Lucia on a barely blown breath.

We stood there, looking guilty. Then Max walked into the room. "Where are the mushrooms?" The question was calm. As always, his voice had that lilt that made him sound Jamaican, even though he didn't have the dreads to go with it. Max shaved his head because "There's not that much to start with. And because it makes me look tough when I'm boxing." I always thought he looked kind of like a semisweet chocolate Easter egg, but I kept this to myself.

"Mushrooms," I said, because that one I could answer in a positive, responsible way. "Nicholas just left."

Max sighed. "At least ten minutes, then. If Pekar's is open."

"They are," Lucia said. "We came home that way."

"Ah, good." Max turned, and as he went back into the kitchen I heard him say, "Might as well start on the spinach, then," and Tonio said, "Already done. Shall we work on the walnuts, instead?"

Floss was paying no attention to the kitchen conversation. She took measured steps toward us. She moved like a dancer. "No waxed thread? Not one spool?"

"Be right back," I said, walking backward. I slid out the door and left Lucia to deal with Floss.

WHY FLOSS NEEDS TO BE DEALT WITH AND
WHY LUCIA IS THE ONE WHO SHOULD DEAL

Floss is Faerie royalty, and even though she doesn't claim it, sometimes she acts like it.

Floss can be very fierce.

Lucia deals with Floss better than I do. Probably because when she was so sad, Lucia escaped by wishing herself into Faerie. The first time I met her, she and Floss came through together.

Floss really needs the thread. (It was irresponsible

to forget. I hate being irresponsible.) As puppet master, Floss is making breathable flying fish puppets—I don't know, I just know that if Floss is making them, they'll work—and she needs very strong connectors.

So Lucia dealt, and I went out for thread.

III

"Soggy. Wet out."

The rain had decided to be serious by the time I hit the street. And of course I didn't have an umbrella. My cotton sweater, the one that had felt so cozy when we were flyering, soon felt like a piece of chain mail.

But Floss needed thread, and it was truly my fault that I hadn't bought it before the rain decided to cover my world, so I kept squelching through puddles, some up to my ankles, until I got to Knobbe's Stationery shop.

I loved Knobbe's. It smelled of handmade paper and dust. There were rainbows of pens, little rubber stamps and multitone ink pads, book boards, and bins full of spangles that you could mix and match in tiny brown paper bags and then buy by the ounce. There was no reason at all for this shop to be where it was except for the fact that a Knobbe started it when Max's apartment and all its neighbors, for blocks in each direction, were high-tone addresses. The store just didn't leave when everyone else did. People came to the shop from all over the city.

Knobbe III knew me. This was because I was there all the time, except of course when I was supposed to be—e.g., thread for Floss. For me, I just came to breathe the air and dream. I had all kinds of ideas. One day, I'd start making those accordion books and I'd sell them down at Pastimes Square during the weekly market. And Floss had said she knew something about Japanese bindings. I thought I could use those to make blank books. Or I could bind sections together with different colored threads and make memory books.

This time, though, it was waxed thread for the Outlaws.

"Hello, Knobbe Three," I said as I squelched through the door. I wrung out the hem of my sweater, which didn't help at all.

"Soggy," said Knobbe. "Wet out."

Knobbe is often a man of few words.

"Yep." I am sometimes a woman of few words when I'm with him.

"Want something?" he asked.

"Waxed thread, please. Cherry red, sea blue, grass green, sunlight."

Knobbe clicked the spools on his counter, tallied the total in his head, and named his price.

When I got my bag it was much bigger than it needed to be for four spools of thread. Inside there were two 3 x 4 book boards and silky cream paper, perfect for accordion folds.

"Knobbe," I said, touched by the gift, but he waved me off.

"Stay dry" was all he said.

But dry was impossible. The rain was more like a high-pressure cold shower than the screen of water it had been before. I tucked Knobbe's bag under my T-shirt, which was only marginally drier than my sweater, and ran.

By the time I'd made it home, it was obvious that Nicholas and the mushrooms had arrived. The house smelled like a four-star Italian restaurant, and all the voices were coming from the kitchen.

"Wow. Are you wet," Nicholas said when I walked in.

"Really? What a lawyerly observation. Was it the sock prints?"

Nicholas grinned.

I shook myself, feeling like a large dog, gave Floss her thread, and checked my boards and paper. Satisfied that they were intact, I said, "I'm just going to go get rid of these sixteen extra pounds of water," and headed for the bathroom and soft, dry towels. Behind me, Tonio yelled, "If you hurry there might still be some food left."

"Thanks," I yelled back, teeth chattering. I knew he was telling me this because of my usual long, hot water—draining showers. Tonio kept trying tricks to break me of this habit. Telling me the food could run out was a good one. I didn't want to miss food, ever.

Showered, I went into the dining room wearing threadbare jeans and a T-shirt that read "Spotted

Dog Records—for the mutt in you." My hair was still wet and tousled because I'd combed it by simply running my fingers through while my head was upside down. Floss, who is always the picture of perfect, sighed at me and shook her head. I smiled back because we both had known from day one that we'd never come even close to an agreement on forms of dress.

Nicholas passed me a beer (dark) and Lucia tossed me a napkin (blue with white elephants) and we all sat down at the stretchy table in Max's dining room. We ate pizza, and we talked, and that was when the trouble started.

Through a mouthful of pizza Lucia said, "While Persia and I were hanging the flyers, I read them."

"Congratulations," said Floss, but she smiled when she said it, which made it seem like a compliment.

Lucia took it just that way and smiled herself. "They should talk more about the wonders of the show," she said. "Persia and I agree."

Tonio glanced at me and I said, "Maybe something that doesn't scream magic. Stars and spangles."

"And flying fish, this time," Lucia added.

"I'll keep that in mind," Tonio said. To Max he added, "Do we even have a fish graphic?"

Max shrugged and said, "We have everything."

"So," Lucia continued, "on the flyer, under 'Place' it says 'You'll know it when you find it.'"

Tonio nodded because he knew exactly what it said. He and Max were the flyer makers, after all. They used funky fonts and old, old computer programs that gave their work a very distinctive look. I could recognize an Outlaw flyer from a block away.

"And really . . . I think that's not so good," Lucia finished in a rush.

Floss's voice was gentle and even when she asked, "And what exactly should it say, then?"

"The place. The actual name or the address or something."

Nicholas glugged his beer. "Kind of defeats a certain purpose, doesn't it?"

"Obscurity?" Lucia asked, and I laughed.

Tonio looked at me again with those beautiful eyes of his, and I shrugged. "Sorry. It was funny."

"It was," he agreed. "But you know why we use those words."

"People find us," Max pointed out as he reached across the table for another piece of broccoli walnut pizza. "Word of mouth and all that."

Lucia, like Nicholas and like me, knew some parts of Tonio and Max's history. By default this also meant we knew parts of the Outlaws' history. Mostly we knew that we kept a low profile because of "past events." I think each of us knew different bits of those past events, but I wasn't positive because we'd never all sat down to put the jigsaw puzzle pieces together. We also knew that we worked with Floss and magic, and that not everyone made allowances for magic, no matter the context or the content.

Lucia agreed that, yes, people found us. But even though she could read undercurrents better than almost anyone, she walked right through them, went over to the other side of the river, and added, "But we'd do better if word of mouth didn't take so long."

"We do just fine," Tonio said, and there was a jaggy edge to his voice.

Nicholas, who had been watching and listening, made the decision to side with Lucia. "She's right, Tonio. I love the Outlaws, you know I do. I wouldn't be here otherwise. But money does grease the wheels. Lately ours have been grinding."

This was Nicholas, remember. I love Nicholas, I think. I love Tonio, too, but it's a very different thing. And extra money would be nice. I admit it—I live hanging on to one end of a very skinny shoestring. It'd be nice to be holding on to a rope instead. So I went with what looked like the winning side. "It's not like money's a bad thing."

Tonio stood up—stood up so fast that his chair scraped the floor and left a nasty scratch in its wake. He stood up with enough of a jerk that the table shimmied. Floss put her half-eaten slice of pizza down very gently and looked wary. But Lucia, even though she looked wretched, stuck to her original idea. "It'd just be nice," she almost whispered, "to see a full house when we open instead of just before we close."

"All right," Tonio said, and his voice was calm. Too calm. Restrained. "Let me make sure that everyone understands just what happens—now—and how it relates to what happened then."

Max shifted in his seat, uneasy. He looked like there might be a fire under his chair.

"Now we put up flyers. Now people who want to find us do. Now word of mouth builds. More people come. By the time anyone who can cause trouble finds out where we are, we're gone. This all works because the troublemakers are slow.

"Then," Tonio continued, in that same flat voice, "we named the place, the date, the time. Then we had bigger crowds. Then I got jailed for being a fey-loving rabble rouser and a magic user, a 'friend of the enemy.'"

The silence in the room was almost loud enough to drown out the noise of the rain.

"I prefer now to then," Tonio said at last, and he left, a half-eaten pizza slice still on his plate.

Max got up to follow him. "Not one of your best performances, everyone," he said over his shoulder.

More silence. Then, "I still think—," Lucia said in a tiny voice, but she was cut off by Floss.

"Don't. Don't think." This was Floss in her steve-dore voice. When she uses it she's never attempting kindness. Whoever else Floss sticks up for, Tonio is always at the top of her list. And since we all know she uses magic, comments about it, especially paired with the word "enemy," make her understandably twitchy.

Lucia never forgot coming here with Floss. That trip was her first point of entry into the Outlaws. She thought of Floss as her ally. When she heard that voice directed at her, she shriveled up like an unwatered plant.

I saw it happen. I saw Floss see it happen, too. Relationships have never seemed to be one of Floss's strong points. They fluster her. It makes me wonder just how things work in Faerie.

Floss looked at Lucia, growled under her breath, and flickered out of the room. Lucia gulped on what sounded like a sob, shoved her chair back so hard it toppled, and disappeared in her turn, although she just went around a wall and into the kitchen. I could hear her slamming pots into the sink.

Nicholas and I sat alone, the remains of the pizza mute witness to everything that had happened. We sat, and I, at least, listened to the rain.

When the sun comes out the whole world looks better. This is especially true after an evening of disorder and discontent. Unfortunately, it was still raining the next morning.

Max and Tonio were back though, crumbling muffins around the living room and drinking coffee the way they always did, with enough cream to cause a heart attack on the spot. Nicholas had gone back to his dorm room once we'd made something of an effort to clean up the dining room, and he hadn't yet shown up for the day. Lucia was nowhere to be seen, Floss was working, and I was aimless. Now that the flyers were up, and possibly pulp with all the moisture in the air, I was waiting for rehearsals to start. This wouldn't happen until Floss finished her latest creation, which involved lots of faux feathers and swearing and no magic at all.

"Coffee?" Max asked me when I wandered by. I

sighed like a drama queen and shook my head.

"Muffin?" Tonio tried, and I shook my head again.

"I'm bored," I muttered. "Bored and looking for excitement."

"Don't bother," Tonio said, his voice dry and flat. "It's never as good as you think it'll be."

"Probably not," I agreed, "but neither is doing nothing."

Floss came into the room. She looked like an enlarged bird. Yellow and blue and spring green feathers followed her like stray puppies. She was blowing air toward her forehead, but the feathers she seemed to be trying to dislodge fluttered prettily, then settled back into her hair and dangled.

"I think," she said between breaths, "I'm through. Anyone want to take a look?"

"Me," I said before Tonio or Max could think. "I want to take a look."

Floss jerked her head back the way she'd come. Two feathers floated down, one catching on her eyebrow. "Damn," she growled.

"Why don't you just pull them off?" I asked. "It

looks like they're driving you crazy."

Floss held out the hands that had been tucked in the pockets of the scraggy green jacket she wore as her work smock. She looked like she was wearing feathered gloves.

"Oh," I said, making a futile attempt to brush the things away. After three tries I said, "Did you glue them to yourself on purpose?"

Floss narrowed her eyes. "What do you think?"

"I think you're a mess," I said as I shook feathers around the room.

It was probably the green feather in his coffee that made Tonio sigh and say, "Let's see the creature, Floss."

We walked in a small parade accompanied by feather confetti. I found Lucia as soon as I turned the corner into Floss's workroom. She was modeling an egg-shaped, sassy chicken suit, as big around as three or four Lucias put together. Her legs, in green striped stockings, came out of the bottom, and her head, dressed in a fetching little blue feather cap, came out the top. She had big rubber-toed shoes on her feet, and yellow rubber kitchen gloves on her hands. It was a charming and, at the same time, completely absurd bird.

"A spangled vest," Tonio suggested.

"And long glitter eyelashes," said Max.

"Eyelashes. Ugh," said the Lucia-bird.

Floss stood there, arms crossed, feathers fluttering around her, and narrowed her eyes. "I like the vest idea," she said at last. "In red, maybe, or is that too contrasty? But I'm not set on the eyelashes."

"Good." Obviously this was from Lucia.

Since I hadn't contributed much, I said, "If you do the red on the vest, make the spangles green and yellow," which made Floss shudder and say, "Stick with book building, my dear."

I laughed and said, "Just trying to do my part."

Floss said, "Umph," but I could tell her mind wasn't really on her response. She was off in creativity land. Getting her out of there was even harder than getting her to talk about Faerie.

IV

"Total chaos and incredulity."

*W*e all pretended that Lucia hadn't said anything about venues, and we moved ahead with plans for *The Bastard and the Beauty*. We worked like devils. We worked like crazy. Sometimes, when Floss was particularly amazed at the amount of work being accomplished, she said we worked like brownies.

"Brownies," Nicholas would echo, "or beginning law students." He only said this because he was stuck on a case involving a plastic surgeon and a previously wrinkled old man. When anyone asked how it was progressing, he just sighed and then said, "Please let me be the evil villain. I just want to pummel someone. Or something."

This always made Tonio laugh until Nicholas glared little shooting stars at him, so Tonio finally gave in. Nicholas was now spending every free minute rehearsing the part of the Bastard.

I was completely on Nicholas's side because I'd been picked to play the Beauty. Don't get excited here, even though I was. I wasn't picked because I was so stunning. I was picked because I was the least stage-inhibited female around.

Lucia would work any puppet in the world or be in any kind of costume as long as she didn't have to be very verbal.

Floss preferred, and was needed, to adjust costumes and make trees walk and fish fly. People who came to our shows as Outlaw virgins were consistently amazed by Floss's artistry, and rightly so, because although she used magic to bring things to the peak of their goodness, without the artistry all the magic in the world wouldn't have made a difference.

PUPPETS THAT MAY MAKE AN APPEARANCE AT
AN OUTLAW SHOW

Walking mountains
Floating planets
Suns the size of marbles
Sparrows big enough to be ridden across a stage
Frog heads as large as supersize helium balloons
And, of course, fish that breathe

Think of all this visual overload happening at once and you've got an idea, if you haven't seen us yet, of the scope of an Outlaw production. It all made something that was wonderful, magical, and, more often than not, highly political and rude. Previous Outlaw shows include *Rape and Ruin*, *Flirting with Foster, Quotes They Say They've Never Said,* and now, *The Bastard and the Beauty.*

Once Nicholas became Bastard, I became even more committed to my part than normal. We got an onstage kiss, too. I worked toward that, and then worked it for all I was worth, even though it was obvious that the kiss would end in certain death.

So what was *The Bastard and the Beauty* about? Tonio started a lot of our plays with fairy tales, those stories couched in hidden messages about the proper way for people, especially young ladies, to behave. Moralistic little tales about people who don't do what they're "supposed to do" and how they pay for the fact that they ignore consequences. For this particular production, he gave magic free rein. Viewers would watch the Beauty try to make the Bastard do the right thing, watch him ignore her, watch people turn into animals, and watch everyone pay for the mistakes of others.

Tonio's imagination, perspective, and worldview constantly amaze me.

And the giant chicken? Well, in a tale with this many turns and detours, who better to have for your narrator?

Remember, though, Lucia was in that costume, and Lucia, gifted as anyone I've ever seen with comic timing and pratfalls, didn't like to talk onstage. So Tonio played the voice and Lucia acted out the narration.

Total chaos and incredulity.

I love the Outlaws.

COMPLETE EXPLICATION INTERLUDE
The Bastard and the Beauty, a Cautionary Tale

He's a lawn boy at a golf course located in an exclusive country club, the one with the chicken mascot. His job is to spray noxious chemicals on everything. One day he meets a rich, lovely young lady (me!) who begs him to stop. "The fish are dying," she says, pointing to a pretty incongruous koi pond near the sixteenth hole.

"They're fish," he tells her. "Just fish. If these die, the owners get more. Besides, I'm only doing my job."

He's rough and he's tough, but it's plain to see that he thinks she's pretty hot. Still, no matter what she says, he won't budge.

"It's my job. I do what they tell me."

As you're picturing this in your mind, imagine those breathing puppet fish worked by Floss from a rigging, flying and dying all over the stage, and small puppet golfers stepping around and through the golden orange bodies.

Beauty points out the carnage. Bastard turns away, just like the golfers. But she keeps working at it, at him. He's more taken with her every time he sees her, and to reflect this, her costumes get more and more dramatic in color (shades of orange and gold) as the play progresses.

Finally he gets up the nerve to ask her out for dinner at the golf course clubhouse. Of course she says yes because just as he's attracted to her, she's attracted to him, even though she hates his job.

During dinner, dead koi float by the window like fish on parade. He pretends not to see. She almost cries. When she's so upset that she spills her soup, he tries to dab at her thigh with a damp napkin. She screams, leaps up, and runs outside. He follows. She's heading straight for the sixteenth green, for the pond. He yells, "Stop!

Stop! I sprayed just today. Don't go near the water!"

She throws one anguished look over her shoulder and then stumbles as her legs disappear and become a split bow tail.

She throws herself into the pond, her golden dress torn off to show scales, but as soon as she hits the water she rises, gasping, to the surface, then turns belly-up and dies. (I don't have to do all of this—thank goodness for Floss's puppet magic.)

The last scene is the lawn boy destroying all his spraying equipment.

"I like to think of that as being similar to the last scene of *Hamlet*," Tonio always said during rehearsals. Then he'd grin while we kind of groaned because, really, a koi compared to the Prince of Denmark? Everyone knows Hamlet was pretty nutty, while I, as the human koi, was only pointing out the dangers of antienvironmentalism.

While Floss perfected her puppets, I made books. This was something I did in my spare time. And why? Because I loved how they looked and felt in my hands. I loved the possibility of the blank pages, the anticipation, I guess. But here's the most dax thing about it: I loved the usefulness. It was like a tool that I could customize to do almost anything.

My hobby had morphed into something I did for the Outlaws, too. One of my contributions to any Outlaw production was true, bound programs. This was something I'd never seen in any other troupe— little hardbound books that passed through the audience before they got the paper programs that they took home. I always made at least three of these books and then designed the take-homes around my original. My books held cast lists, behind-the-scenes stuff, the plot line—things like that all wrapped up in a unique little package that looked and felt special. Most people seemed very impressed.

I had the board that Knobbe III gave me on the night of rain and pizza. I had atmospheric singer-songwriter music strolling through Max's apartment.

I had two mismatched pieces of cloth, filched from Floss, a pot of glue that was nothing like the paste we use to hang posters, and I was planning the programs for B&B (that's *Bastard and the Beauty*).

When I was done I knew Tonio would look at my books and say, "I knew you had vision."

Max would say, "Beautiful, darling."

Lucia would say, "I like it. Really. But I wish you could do those accordion things," which I was working on, but they were trickier than you'd think.

Nicholas would toss one in the air to check for structural integrity and then approve when it didn't fall to pieces.

And Floss? Floss would say, "I hope you didn't cut that cloth off of anything. I hope you're using scraps."

So no matter where I got that cloth, I always nodded in a fierce and positive way because no one messed with Floss. No one.

V

"Sage and Damen."

*O*ur flyers said "Place: You'll know it when you find it."

Tonio and Max were on the prowl, looking for the Place. Nicholas had already scouted his campus and found a lovely little grove near the bridge over the Tamsan River. Nicholas tried to convince him, but Tonio wasn't sure about staging on the campus of a private school. "But the bridge," Nicholas told us, "is perfect for those scenes when Bastard strides forcefully into the distance."

There are many quotation marks here, both internal and external. "Strides forcefully into the distance" is a stage direction. Nicholas loved to speak in stage. When he did, it was very cute. When anyone else tried it, I shook my head and sighed. But even though Nicholas had used stage talk, proving he was deeply involved in the production, Tonio said no. In a way I thought this was too bad, because I knew that bridge. It had a Japanese air and seemed like it would be just right dangling over the koi pond.

Floss had scouted Faerie. So far, we'd never done even one day of a production there, but Floss always looked. She'd come back with oblique comments. "I found a good spot, but there was too much blood on the grass." Or, "I thought the stream under the Musical Bridge would work perfectly, but I'd forgotten about that hole in the middle."

When this happened everyone looked at Lucia, because sometimes she went along on Floss's scouting expeditions. Lucia always just nodded. Floss said, "Internecine wars," shook her head, and wandered off to look for something. Possibly green rhinestones.

I stayed away from location scouting. I didn't think I had what it took since most chosen sites, when I first saw them, scared me by their complete uselessness. Later, with everything in place, the lights on and the moon watching us, the damn spots were perfect.

This baffled me, but it was okay. I'd rather make programs.

On Wednesday, though, Tonio and Max came back to the apartment right around dusk and they both looked excited.

"Great, great place," Max said.

Tonio slipped his hand into the crook of Max's elbow and beamed. "Absolutely perfect," he agreed.

"Quiet. Out of the way. Spacious."

"Huge," said Tonio, and he almost crowed.

"Quiet. Out of the way," Lucia echoed. She sounded doleful. "Nobody comes to out of the way. Quiet, maybe. But not out of the way."

"Yes, darling. We know what you think," Tonio said, but he smiled when he said it. "Really, though, this is absolutely right."

Lucia looked doubtful, Nicholas looked interested, and Floss looked at us all through a handful of pink felt and red feathers. I raised my eyebrows and tried to look encouraging. When nothing happened I said, "Do you think you could maybe tell us where this perfect place is?"

"Sage and Damen." This was from Max.

Nicholas frowned. "There's something at Sage and Damen? I can't picture a thing. I mean, I can't picture a thing we can use. Really industrial."

"Perfect place for a romance," Tonio said. "Look at Max and me. We met at a rave in an abandoned warehouse."

"You were probably the only ones who came out of the experience intact," Nicholas muttered. He was wise enough to know that everyone accused of buying or selling wasn't necessarily doing either of those things. He also knew that the sellers weren't always fey. But that didn't make him approve of the users who were so often attracted to rave events. He was no fan of drug culture.

"You wound me," Tonio said, high drama in his voice.

"We weren't drugging, we were clubbing," Max said, his voice dry as old wine. "You know we don't do that stuff."

Tonio took pity on us. "Location: old factory.

Not too big. Lots of electrics."

Nicholas perked up, his love of lighting shining through.

"Easy enough to get to, and get into, but close to a dead end . . ."

"It's legal," Max added, and he grinned. "We can actually afford it for a short run."

"Wait," I said in triumph. "I know. Sage and Damen. The old chocolate factory?"

"Point," Tonio said as he tapped me on the head. "Best of all, it smells like heaven."

"Chocolate." I grinned. We'd come home every night with our clothes wrapped around us like papers twisted over truffles.

"We now," Tonio said in his announcer voice, "have incentive."

Floss sniffed. "We always have had, dear. I'm done. Or I would be if I had three long socks and some Popsicle sticks."

Nicholas put up surreptitious postings from a bogus ConnectNow account at school. Lucia and I put up more surreptitious flyers around town. Max and Tonio wrote a check for the chocolate factory owner, absentee landlord that he was, and before I was ready—way before I was ready—it was space rehearsal time.

The first time I'd heard this term I'd said, "Dress rehearsal, you mean?"

"No, sweetie," Tonio had said. "That comes after. Most people rehearse in their space from day one."

"Which we obviously haven't been doing," Floss had said. She'd pointed to the east and added, "Could you get me a golden sword, please?"

Early in my time at Outlaws questions like this would wallop me. Now I just get the golden sword. Or whatever else Floss wants. The difference is that now I know she means a prop, or a puppet.

WHAT HAPPENS AT SPACE REHEARSAL

We meet the space. While this sounds silly, it's not.

We get used to the space, and it gets used to us. This sounds a little cosmic. Maybe it is.

There is much flurry of activity involving lights and

electrical magic and, of course, real magic, too.
Obviously, that's Floss.
We get things hung and strapped and sequenced and
then start to work on the play.

So, space rehearsal in the chocolate factory. Working there was akin to having someone put dark chocolate creams on your pillow every single night. The ceilings were high enough to hang things and low enough to be acoustic. There was a lovely space where we set up the long, old rows of seats that we'd rented from Fly-By-Nite Theater Supply. There was even a little atrium where Max could set up a box office.

If we hadn't had the heavenly smells and those prime little touches, though, working there would still have been a treat. It was like having a permanent place to set up shop. After a few days I noticed that we were actually leaving flotsam and jetsam in our wake instead of gathering it up and carrying it all home every night.

One night Floss left a few pieces of Lucia's chicken suit behind. Nicholas, who was doing something wonderful and strange with an electrical hookup, yelled, "Floss. Costume."

She looked at him over her shoulder. "What? It's fine. You'll lock up before you leave. That takes care of most of the criminal element on your end. None of my relatives really like breaking down doors. Too much work. That takes care of most of the criminal element on my end. We're fine."

That last bit made me say, "Floss, what does your family do, exactly?"

She shrugged. "Rule things," she said, and I didn't even think she was being vague.

This exchange between Floss and Nicholas, though, was the first time that I realized that we were now involved in a very different kind of Outlaw production. I thought back to the night of rain and pizza and wondered if Lucia's comments had made a difference, after all. I glanced at Tonio, trying not to be obvious. He looked happy, maybe happier than I'd ever seen him. Max walked past me just then and, as if doing some mind-read thing said, "It's good to see him this way. Lucia had a point." Then he went toward Nicholas and threw him an extension cord that was wrapped in so many spirals, it must have been the length of the Amazon.

It was probably the most relaxed few days of space rehearsal we'd ever had. It's amazing what that proper home feel can do for you. When we started dress rehearsals, we already felt two weeks ahead.

Then it was opening night, in only two days. While we hadn't changed our flyers, word was already leaking out. People kept coming by, people we'd never seen, which was gratifying. While we loved our core of Outlaw regulars, new people meant we were doing something right. These new-to-the-Outlaw-experience folks peered through the windows, their fingers and breath making smoke whorls in the dust on the glass. They pushed open doors, and when we asked what they wanted they looked at Lucia's feathers and Floss's clouds and grinned.

"Just checking," they said, and still smiling, they disappeared like snuffed candle flames.

VI

"The reporter from **Nighttimes** *is here."*

pening night. Jitters, jitters. I jumped at the slightest sound. I ignored Max's divine lasagna, a big pan of which was sitting backstage on a plank supported by three milk crates, a pile of wood, and six old books. I ignored pretty much everything except for the vague, sick flutter in my stomach and the desert in my throat. I drank gallons of water, drank so much I was afraid my costume for act 1 (very beauty queen) wouldn't fit, and I was still parched.

Nicholas passed me at one point, stopped, took the pint glass out of my hand with gentle fingers, and said, "Persia. You know it's going to be fine."

I grabbed the glass back like a drowning woman

grabbing for her life preserver, gulped more water, and nodded. "Right. I know this. I just thought it'd be good if my throat didn't close up. Because of dryness. I thought I should be able to speak."

There was wonder in his eyes. "I don't think I've seen you like this before. You usually project calm and level. Sort of mellow, even."

"Nicholas," I said distinctly, "before I was never corseted into a prom dress and expected to be cute."

He looked at me, his eyes flowing up and down my dress like a confused river, then he leaned in and kissed me on the nose. "You're always cute," he said as he walked away.

"Hmm," said Lucia. She stepped into my view frame and blocked Nicholas's back. There was a wicked smile on her face. "Nicholas and Persia sitting in a tree . . ."

"Oh, for God's sake, Lucia. Grow up," I muttered. I stomped away, but I have to admit that in spite of my nervousness, and the shyness that seemed to be a product of Lucia's rhyme, I was grinning.

Costume pieces came together. Props were

gathered. Floss, stevedore voice in full swing, ordered everyone around, even Tonio. He behaved exactly as she wanted and never said one word. The clock ticked on. Max disappeared to take tickets. Floss made last-minute cloud adjustments. Lucia put on her chicken feet. Nicholas pulled down on the bill of his baseball cap and looked tough. Tonio cleared his throat and tapped lightly on his backstage mike, then went to check the speakers out front. And I pretended I was a socialite.

Tonio flipped switches, the lights blinked, the curtain (one very large marshmallow cloud in Day-Glo pink) rose, and we were off.

By the time we were done we'd survived a minor electrical fire and one broken mike, but those were the only stumbling blocks. Everything else went exactly as planned. Puppets walked, suns rose, even the silly fountain in act 2 sprayed water where and when it was supposed to. And the applause—oh, fury, the applause was loud and long and more than I'd ever heard for an Outlaw opening night.

When the audience was gone, when the house

lights were up, when we all looked at one another with pleased expressions—that was when Max swung his arm around Lucia's shoulder and planted a kiss on her cheek. "Brilliant, kiddo. An Outlaw home." He fanned out the night's takings. "Good people. Good money."

Then he grabbed Tonio. "And to you—good call. You listened. You acted. You overcame. I love you."

Lucia grinned and bumped shoulders with Floss. I, emboldened by the night's events, leaned over and kissed Nicholas on the ear. He looked confused, then swept me into a Bastardly embrace and squeezed. Happy Outlaws. The world seemed to be a perfect place.

Three nights after the opening Nicholas skidded backstage and said, "The reporter from *Nighttimes* is here. Front row." He looked like he'd arranged the appearance personally.

Tonio stopped moving. "Major is here?"

"I don't know Major," Nicholas said, "but I know it's *Nighttimes*. I've seen him around before, always at new shows. It's been awhile. But I know he's from *Nighttimes*," he added fairly, "because his bag has the logo on the side."

"Maybe he won the bag. Maybe it's a fund-raising promo. Maybe he likes seeing new shows," Max said, but he sounded a little desperate.

"And maybe it's Major," Tonio said, his voice flat.

Nicholas can pick up vibes like a champion. "This was supposed to be good news, you know?"

But Floss shook her head. "Pretty much the exact opposite, I'd say."

I watched everyone. Lucia shrugged, Nicholas seemed confused, but Floss, Tonio, and Max looked like the hounds of hell were chomping on their heels.

"What's going on?" I asked.

"Major is what's going on," said Tonio. His voice was dark and weary. "Major's not a friend of mine."

"I thought he was gone," Max said. "Didn't you say he was gone?"

"I did. I just never mentioned that he came back." Tonio sighed. "I was hoping he'd turn out to be something we wouldn't have to deal with."

"You knew?" Max sounded incredulous. Tonio shrugged, a bone-tired gesture.

"Major," Floss said. The word seemed bitter in her mouth. "He used to follow me like an acolyte, asking questions about magic, about Faerie. He even tried to follow me home once. To my Faerie home." She stopped and her shoulders shivered. "Almost made it, too. Very scary. Mortals should not be able to just waltz into Faerie."

"That was his flirtatious side. And if he was trying to get into Faerie he couldn't have been waltzing. He was probably running like hell." Tonio almost smiled at what must have been a mental picture of Major doing that run.

Floss snarled.

"He had that huge, galloping crush on you. He was trying to show appreciation and admiration." Now Tonio sounded like he was making a halfway effort to be conciliatory, but the effort didn't work. Floss glared at him and inhaled heavily.

"I know," he said, and he shrugged. "I never said it was a good thing."

"Major," Max repeated. "There was also that little incident when he tried to have me arrested for running a pixie dust gang."

"Because if he couldn't have me, he wanted you, and you weren't interested," Tonio said, toneless now. "And also because he figured hurting you was a great way to get back at me. It was complete stupidity. It shows just how twisted his brain is. He didn't have even half of one leg to stand on, and he knew it."

Max grunted.

"I just said *Nighttimes*. I didn't say Major anything," Nicholas reminded anyone who was listening.

"Didn't have to. I know exactly who's covering theater for *Nighttimes*. He's just so anti-Outlaw that I didn't think he'd bother to show up, even if we did go more or less mainstream. The only reason he ever checked out one of our productions was to make rude, suggestive comments about magic and to try to make it sound like we were consorting with the criminal element in Faerie. I guess I'd hoped he was over that."

"Wishful thinking. It hardly ever works," Max said. He sounded apologetic.

Tonio nodded. "But it's nice to hope." Almost as an afterthought he added, "And he didn't get back till after we'd leased this building."

"Wait," I said. "All the 'You'll Know It When You Find It' stuff—you've been hiding from one guy? I mean, just one guy?"

"He's got a lot of pull for just one guy," Max said, grim.

"He's amazingly vindictive," Floss added.

"He knows the right people, too," Tonio said. "He knows how easy it is to get someone in trouble. He works loopholes like nobody I've ever met before."

Nicholas, Lucia, and I stood there like a group excluded from a party. We listened. And apparently not one of us knew what to say next because we clumped together like mimes looking for something to mime about.

The timer we used as a ten-minute reminder binged. It sounded like it was a very long way away. Lucia jumped the smallest bit. Nicholas said, almost to himself, "I'm getting pretty good at loopholes," but his voice was a low shadow of normal, and no one reacted to his comment.

Floss sighed. "Ten minutes," she said. "Make it count."

In spite of Major, in spite of the gloom-and-doom scenario that I still didn't really understand, we put on a good show. The audience seemed to love us, which is at least half the reason for putting on a show, after all. (The other half, I guess, is the sheer giddiness of a good performance, and the ability to overcome all of those little niggling fears that hide in the sides of your mind.)

Two productions ago we'd started an audience participation segment on the nights when it felt right. This consisted of opening up our secrets backstage and inviting in onlookers. Why Tonio decided that the night Major was there was a good one for this I still don't understand. Apparently, Max didn't understand either.

"Not tonight. Really. Not tonight," he said to Tonio.

"He won't come," Tonio said in a voice edged with scorn.

"And if he does?"

"There is nothing," Tonio responded, in hard, precise words, "he can do to me."

"That he hasn't done before?" Max asked. It could have been a taunt, but his voice was too gentle for that. "Why court it?"

"I know what I can and can't do. What I should and shouldn't do," Tonio snapped. "I don't need an over-the-hill boxer telling me how to handle my life."

The gasp by my ear came from Lucia. "Persia," she whispered. "Do something. Make them stop."

I understood exactly what Lucia meant. Tonio saying something cruel to Max was unheard of. Ever since I'd known them they'd talked together, laughed together, even fought together, but I'd never before heard this kind of rudeness. And I'd certainly never heard purposefully hurtful words flung from one of them to the other.

I glanced at Lucia. She looked beaten and cowed, as if someone were chasing her with a large stick.

I said, "Lucia. Go find Nicholas. Bring him back here."

She looked at me with eyes as huge and shiny as new coins. "Lucia," I said again, and this time I shook her shoulder. "Can you find Nicholas? Please?"

She blinked twice, in pairs, and then ran off to stage right. I stood where I was and breathed slow, even breaths until Nicholas, still dressed in his lawn boy garb, came running back with Lucia. By this time Tonio had stalked off. After a moment Max turned 180 degrees and walked, tall and proud, in the opposite direction. I grabbed at Nicholas, my hands landing just above his wrists. "How much do you know about Tonio's stint in prison?" I asked.

"Not much." He shook his head, but his eyes were serious, so I figured he knew something.

"But what?" I pressed.

"Tonio never talked about it," Nicholas hedged.

"Fine," I growled. "What did Max say, then?"

"Persia, really. I don't want to say. Anything I think I know is put together with guesswork and glue."

Lucia chirped, a cross between a cry and a groan. Both Nicholas and I twisted around to look at her. Her eyes were back to that shiny coin shape and she looked like she wanted to run. I was glad Floss wasn't nearby, because if she had been, I think Lucia might have grabbed her and tried to go to Faerie to get away from this anxiety that seemed to be holding all of us locked tight in its fist.

"Lucia?" I asked.

"Max said this one time that it was a political thing," Lucia whispered. "That they were doing a pro-test kind of a play outside of some big meeting . . ."

"A trade-versus-the-environment summit," Nicho-las said, and the words sounded like they were being pulled out of his throat. "That part I'm pretty positive about."

"Right. Okay," said Lucia, her voice still so soft that I had to lean in to catch everything. "Anyway, someone called the police."

"Major," said Floss. She must have flown in because I sure hadn't heard her footsteps. And I didn't even think she could fly. "Major called. Said we were dis-turbing the peace. Said we were antigovernment, anti-jobs, anti-rights-of-the-people. Said we were performing without a permit and that we were using fey magic in our permitless performance."

"In other words," Max finished, embellishing Floss's point—and I hadn't heard him, either, which made me shake my head and try to clear my ears—"he said anything he could think of to get us, Tonio especially, in trouble. And he kind of yanked the whole concept of freedom of speech and the right to protest right out from under us at the same time."

I waited for more. When nothing came I tried to break things down into their respective parts. "Let me understand this," I started. "First, the magic part. Wouldn't that have put Floss in trouble too? Why was Tonio the only one to get hauled away?"

"Thank you, Persia," Floss muttered.

"No, I'm just trying to understand," I protested, but at the same time Max looked hard at me and said, "Who's the artistic director? Who's in charge? Who's the one who allowed the 'scourge from the other side'?"

I winced and Floss looked deflated.

Max saw both our reactions, but it was Floss he was talking to when he said, "I didn't mean it. You do know that, right?"

"Of course I do," Floss said. "I was just remembering."

"And the permit?" I persisted. "Did you have one of those?"

"Not that I recall," Max said. "But then neither did any of the twenty or so other groups that were gathered outside the gates and protesting right along with us."

"What happened to them?" When Nicholas asked his question he had law in his voice.

"Not one damn thing," Max said, and his words held the bitterness of unsweetened chocolate.

As if it were his fault, Nicholas said, "I'm sorry." He sounded sad now, but Max just shrugged.

"So the permit thing wasn't really legitimate," I said in clarification, "but they were right about the magic."

"They couldn't prove the magic," Max said, "so that just sort of faded away. But the permit thing—it took awhile to make a case showing that we were the only ones being strong-armed. And during that while, Tonio got to see exactly how the justice system worked from the prison side of things."

"And that was bad?" I guessed.

"Spectacularly bad," Max assured me. "Keep that in mind. Don't ever do anything that could get you locked up."

I looked at him, looked at Floss and Tonio, too. "But aren't we?" My voice was jittery. "Don't we do that with our plays? I mean, there's magic, and we're sure beating up the government and government policies."

"Why do you think we're usually on the move?"

"We're not exactly on the move right now," I pointed out, and I knew I sounded upset.

Max glanced toward Tonio, where he sat alone in a corner. "I hadn't thought we needed to be. Not anymore. Most anti-fey stuff has been directed toward the pixie dust, and the pink and purple drinks, at least lately. We're small. We're mostly under the radar." He hesitated, and added, "I didn't know about Major."

Then Max switched voices so quickly I wondered why he never acted in any production. "And now," he said, "we have visitors."

We all smiled, just like wound-up little mechanical men, and turned to face our audience. Under my breath I said, "Why am I the only one who didn't know any of this?"

Nicholas hissed, "Hush," and we began a whole new performance.

Floss showed off clouds and flying koi. Nicholas showed lighting effects. Lucia walked around in her chicken suit. I talked about the intricacies of making programs and I was pleased that people seemed impressed. (I only mention this because it seemed like the best thing that happened to me all night.)

Max talked about riggings and puppets. And Tonio? Tonio sat in a corner, close to the wings, and waited. Max kept throwing worried glances into that corner, but Tonio dodged them all without even trying.

People came and people went. The crowds thinned to a few, to a couple, to none. And then Major came in.

I knew it was Major. Even without the *Nighttimes* logo on his bag I would have known because Nicholas muttered, "That's him."

Somehow, in that huge backstage area that tiny sentence carried like it was miked.

Major heard. He raised one eyebrow in our direction and said, quite clearly, "It is, indeed. Tonio around?" He sounded sort of jolly and not at all dangerous, and the fact that he was wearing a Mexican wedding shirt somehow made the encounter that much more surreal.

Max coughed. Major walked over to him, held out his hand, and said, "Max. Nice to see you again. Especially since you haven't been seen in the ring lately."

The jibe was said just right, with a concern that almost but not quite overshadowed the glee. Max stood completely still, looked at Major's outstretched hand, made no move to take it, and said, "Hello, Major."

Major looked at his hand himself, shrugged, and dropped it down to his side. He cocked that eyebrow again and looked at all of us, one by one, measuring. When he got to Floss he said, "Beautiful as ever," which made Floss snort and turn away. Major shrugged again. When his eyes landed on me he said again, "Tonio around?"

I was rooted to the floor, stuck right in the middle of the feelings tumbling around me. It was like being caught in an earthquake. No matter which way you turned, you'd lose your footing. I tried, and internally

71

rejected, at least ten answers to that innocuous-sounding "Tonio around?" and then I heard Tonio himself. "Oh, for hell's sake, Major. What?" His voice was like dry ice.

"Tonio!" Jovial. Bouncy. Lying. It was way too easy to tell.

"Were you very offended?" Tonio asked as he walked with precise steps across the backstage area that had, in my mind, grown to the size of two or three acres strung together. "Were we politically incorrect enough? Was there just the right amount of magic? Did we give you fodder for your twee little paper?"

"I never thought you'd do it, you know," Major said, ignoring Tonio's questions. "Never thought I'd see you try to go legit. You'll have to change the company name, won't you?" He stopped. He pretended to think. "Ah, I have it. The Little Lawfuls!" And he laughed.

"Thanks so much for coming," Tonio said, with no sincerity at all. "Don't let us keep you. Just leave the same way you came in."

Major took one step forward. "I'll pan it, you know. Nobody will come. You'll lose everything."

"I doubt you've got that much power."

"Put you in jail before, didn't I?"

Tonio winced, but he held his ground. "I'm not as inexperienced now as I was then."

Major drew breath to reply, but before he could say whatever it was that he was going to say, Max took three long strides and stopped in front of Major. He loomed over the other man. "Enough," Max said. "I'm sick of the banter. Go, Major, and do whatever it is you're going to do. It'll either work or it won't. Right now, I don't care. Just go."

Major shot Max a look of pure snake-bite venom. "Protecting your little love. How sweet."

The air was so thick with anger it was hard to breathe. I saw Tonio's hands clench, but other than that he didn't move. Nicholas was bone still. Lucia looked like she was going to cry, and Floss just looked disgusted. Max said simply, "He can protect himself. I just like to be around in case he needs muscle to do more than protect." He moved one step closer, which seemed to make him grow an additional two feet. From where I stood, glued to the floor, I saw

Major shrink back, just the slightest bit. Then, as if it had been his idea all along, he turned on his heel and walked off without even one backward glance.

The tension around us lifted like laundry floating in the air on a stiff breeze. Lucia dropped to the floor and breathed out the breath she must have been holding since Major walked in, and Nicholas, with wonder in his voice said, "What was that, exactly?"

Tonio sighed. It sounded like the wind in a hollow cave. He didn't look at Max, but it was obvious that he was asking him when he said, "Should I tell them?"

"You probably have to, after a cryptic question like that." Max was by Tonio now, not Major, and his demeanor changed to match the situation. "It's not," he added in a very gentle tone, "going to change anyone's opinion on anything."

Tonio sighed again. "That, Nicholas," he said, "was my ex-lover."

VII

"Faerie's an amazing place.
You should go sometime."

We were back at Tonio and Max's apartment. The room was filled with questions, but Nicholas was the only one chasing the answers.

"That much animosity over a broken affair?" he asked. "There's got to be something more." Nicholas had been saying the same thing, with variations, since we'd locked the chocolate factory and started the long walk home through streets greasy with skimmed rain, streets that matched the way we all felt: flat, slippery, and grungy with odd thoughts instead of old oil.

Tonio sighed. "There's also the fact that he's power hungry like no one I've ever seen, but in this case I

75

really do think it was the fact that I left him. I don't think he'd ever been left before. I think, instead, he always did the leaving. It was probably," he finished, in what I was sure was an understatement, "something of a shock."

Floss, apparently fed up with Nicholas and possibly the rest of us as well, said, "For Mab's sake, Nicholas. Think your age. Spurned love is one of the greatest reasons for wars, killings, displacements. . . ." She stopped. She looked at us all in turn. "That's true here, right? It certainly is in Faerie, so I just assumed . . ." She stopped talking again and looked uncertain. Uncertainty was a look that I rarely saw on Floss's face.

"Of course it is," Tonio answered, interrupting her stumbled statement. "Read some history, Nicholas. Get your head out of those law books."

"He's right, though," I said, loyal to Nicholas. "I mean, getting you arrested? Giving you a record? Sending you to prison? Just because you don't want to go out anymore?" I shook my head, amazed. "Then he throws an attack at Max. Even more then, he tries to get Floss in trouble about magic, which certainly wasn't going to win him any points or make her succumb to his charms."

"Of which he has none," Floss muttered. "And he wasn't truly interested in me. I would have just been a way to get at Tonio."

"It just all sounds so extreme," I continued.

"Helen of Troy," Floss said.

"You know about her?" I asked.

Floss rolled her eyes, a very exaggerated roll. "Persia, please. She was fey, after all."

"I knew about some others, but not her," Lucia said. "You're sure about Helen?"

"I just said," Floss growled. "But if you think about it, you'll see I'm right. What mortal could do what she did?" And she nodded her head as if she'd just laid down a red royal flush.

"Wait. That's really interesting." Nicholas was obviously intrigued. "Is there anyone else from Faerie who's famous?"

Floss shrugged. "Oh, Titiana and Ariel, but you probably already guessed that, they're so obvious. Shakespeare loved us. Queen Elizabeth, the first one. But fey from here?" She thought for a minute. "Hmmm. Well, Susan B. Anthony. Abraham Lincoln. John Wilkes Booth, too, but he played for the other side."

"You have got to be kidding," Nicholas said.

Floss shook her head. "Lots of actors, writers, painters, too, from everywhere. Arty folks. Monet. Gauguin. I've always suspected Beethoven, myself. Definitely Andy Warhol. Cheap Trick. The Beatles. Well, at least John and Paul. Neil Gaiman."

"Okay, I'll buy the historical figures because who can prove it isn't true?" Nicholas nodded, then added, "And because it makes sense, actually. But the Beatles and Gaiman? Cheap Trick? Contemporary people, famous people who fly the fey flag? Kind of dangerous, no?"

"What flag do I fly, then?" Floss's voice was cold and flat as a fresh ice floe.

Nicholas shrugged. "What I said, and what I said wasn't anything against you. You know that. But look at us. Outlaw Puppet Troupe. Why have we been running for so long if everything was fine?"

Floss made a noncommittal noise.

"Probably if you're really famous and you're fey you've got some kind of magical protection to keep you safe," I said. "And probably you don't flaunt it."

Floss grinned at me like I'd correctly identified the phrase from a game of hangman with only three letters on the board. "Exactly," she said.

Max and Tonio were huddled in a corner paying no attention to us, but Lucia had obviously been following the famous-fey conversation. "Faerie's an amazing place. You should go sometime. Floss could take you—could take all of us."

Nicholas and I looked at each other. Max stopped talking to Tonio. Tonio looked at Lucia. Then everyone turned to Floss.

Max spoke in slow measured words. "A hidey-hole if we need one. That's not a bad idea."

Tonio jiggled his shoulders.

Lucia seemed pleased with her suggestion.

Nicholas said simply, "Aarugh," which made him sound like he was a comic book character in dire circumstances.

And I looked straight at Floss and asked, "Could you really do that? Take us"—and here I waved my hand around the room, sort of figuratively pulling us together—"across just like that?" (Finger snap.)

"I could." But I thought she sounded put-upon. Or grudging. She confirmed that when she said, "But in spite of Lucia's views, Faerie may not be where you need to go."

I remembered Floss's oblique comments when she came back from scouting locations. Blood. Holes in the bridges. I remembered her remark about how her family, "ruled things." And I thought that maybe she wasn't put-upon. Maybe she was right.

"We don't have to decide right now, do we?" I let my eyes travel around the room. "We don't really have to do anything right now. We just have to wait and see if we have to do something."

When no one answered I nodded in an encouraging way and said, "Right?"

"Right," Floss said, stevedore voice loud and fine. "Persia's right. Let's just wait and see."

"The show's just starting to roll," Tonio said, and

he sounded strong and sure.

Max said, "Absolutely," and he sounded as strong as Tonio.

Lucia looked embarrassed. "I didn't mean to say a wrong thing," she whispered.

Floss draped an arm around her shoulders. "You didn't. It's always good to examine the possibilities."

And Nicholas? He just shook his head and said, "Go to Faerie. Good hell. What an idea."

But the way he said the last sentence was almost a question, and I wondered what he was really thinking.

VIII

"You've been listening to the street talk, right?"

$\mathcal{T}$he review for *The Bastard and the Beauty* came out in *Nighttimes* on Wednesday. Comments like "flat story line," "uninspired acting," "magic too real to be safe," and "forgettable costumes" were laughable, especially when we compared them with those from the other theater critics. From them we got things like "brilliant set design and costuming," "beautiful magical impressions," "moralism without didacticism," and "enjoyable acting."

"Makes you wonder just how long he thinks he'll hold on to his job this time," Tonio said, and he laughed a laugh that held just as much wickedness as humor.

"He didn't lose it last time," Max pointed out. "He just left."

"He would have lost it if he'd stayed," Tonio said.

Max glanced up from the salad he was mixing. Pears and walnuts and blue cheese. "So you say," he said.

"But it's ridiculous," Nicholas said from where he was sprawled over the papers. "Uninspired acting? Please. I thought I was brilliant."

"So you say." I repeated Max's line and nudged Nicholas's foot with my own. Lucia giggled. But Nicholas knew I was kidding because, truth be told, I'd thought he was brilliant too. And not just his acting. Although you might say I was biased.

However Major's review helped or hindered his career, it didn't affect our crowds. We were playing to sold-out houses now. We had a waiting list. Max even had to get a new computer program to manage ticket sales, and the computer to go with it. Lucia went shopping with him. They went to Omar's Office Emporium and swung an incredible deal.

When they brought home the bags of boxes, stuffed full of equipment and loads of twisty little wires, I said, "Lucia, how do you know what goes with what?" and waggled my fingers at the stacks and piles on the dining room table.

Lucia looked up from where she was sorting a few hundred cables. "Persia, what are you talking about? This is easy. It'll all be ready to go in half an hour." She looked at me, head down and eyes up, and made a "tsk" sound before she went back to work.

I "tsked" myself and went to make more pass-around programs. No computer necessary. All nice, comfy handwork. My originals were wearing, and the nightly crowds were getting too large for three books to make their way through it before intermission. I was beginning to look at loss analysis, and I assumed, purely by the law of either 1) averages or 2) supply and demand, that I was going to come out at least one program short one of these evenings.

On my way out the door to get supplies at Knobbe's, I passed Floss in the living room. She was wrapped in mastic, stalking through feathers and old newspapers and muttering, "Chickens just don't last the way they're supposed to."

I was very happy.

"Hello, Knobbe Three," I sang out as I walked into the store.

The face he turned toward me was worried. "Persia," he said with care. "How's the play going? I saw it early on."

"You didn't tell me," I said. "I would have made a fuss. And a special program, just for you."

"Exactly why."

I sighed and Knobbe III actually grinned. "I liked it. Cutting without being stupid or cloying. Good social commentary. Great puppets. Good-feeling magic."

I beamed at him. "Knobbe Three, thank you."

He tilted his head, a small nod, but he was back to looking worried.

"You've been listening to the street talk, right?" He dropped his question in the air on a delicate exhale.

I fanned some pieces of backing board. "Not so

much, really. I've been pretty busy, after all."

"Maybe you should start."

My hands stopped moving. My eyes stopped scanning decorative cover papers. And I said, "Okay, I'll bite. Why should I start listening to what's being said on the street?"

"Some bad stuff circulating around out there."

"Well, sure. There always is."

"About the play," he added.

"What are you talking about? We're selling out. We've got a waiting list for tickets. We had to buy a new computer, for Mab's sake." I'd adopted Floss's line and found it to be continually useful.

"That may well be," Knobbe III said. "But I've been hearing rumors. Pixie dust everywhere you look, courtesy of the Outlaws. Lots of drinks, most of them pink, but some of them red. Both of those guaranteed to make you wake up with no idea of where you've been or how you got there. Special effects that reek of a fey hand." He watched me, his eyes digging in deep, and added, "Too fey. Too illegal. Too scary."

I pulled out the middle comment. "There are degrees of legality? Isn't something either legal or not?" I asked, but really, I wasn't waiting for an answer. I was thinking about people versus fey and wondering what Knobbe's views were on the subject. It wasn't something we'd ever talked about, but I knew that didn't mean that he had no opinion. *Everyone* had an opinion.

PREVALENT VIEWS ON THE FEY KINGDOM

Members of Faerie are aberrations. We don't want them here, mixing with our own.

Everything in Faerie is love and flowers. (Sometimes I worry more about these people than the previous ones.)

Magic is evil; its practitioners are worse. There are laws about this, and laws are here to protect us.

We're all descended from the fey; we just need to tap into our hidden powers.

They're people, just like everyone else, with the same foibles and problems. They just happen to be able to do magic.

Knobbe III could fall anywhere on the continuum. Just because he'd said he liked the magic in *B&B* didn't mean he liked magic, or the fey.

I knew Floss, and I knew her magic. I knew she wasn't evil, and I knew she wasn't a saint. Because of this I thought of the fey as being more like good old Uncle Mike, or Great-Aunt Honey: normal, with normal ups and downs. But with all these conflicting ideas living in my town, with crazies trying to pass laws about the "separation of us and them," I didn't talk about Faerie with just anyone. Knobbe III didn't exactly fall into the category of just anyone, but I was still smart enough to walk carefully. "You believe what you hear?" I was standing by his counter now, close enough to touch him.

Knobbe III looked at me, really looked for the first time, I think, since I'd known him. Eyes straight into my soul, it felt like. "I believe you're probably using magic, and I don't care at all. Other people might not feel the same way. Pixie dust and colored drinks? That I don't believe a word of. You're all too smart to play around with the kind of people, or fey, who'd be involved in that kind of junk." There was a pause, then he added, "But there's more dust and more drink floating around than there's ever been. Don't act like you haven't noticed. It's like an epidemic."

He was right about that. Just today, on my way over here, I'd passed two people between Max's and Knobbe's who were shaky, wobbly, and aimless. Not scary really, but you could never be sure how things might spin. I could only agree with Knobbe, so I nodded. Then, in case it wasn't clear what I was agreeing with, I added, "But dust and drink—none of that's coming from us."

"I just said I knew it wasn't. Pay attention. That doesn't mean you can ignore the chatter."

"What am I supposed to do about rumors?"

He coughed once and shook his head. "Persia, you're intelligent. You're street-smart. And you're artistic, which means you've got imagination. Put that all to work and then you can tell me what I mean."

I got it then. Of course I did. I probably had before and just hadn't wanted to admit it.

"I should tell Tonio to watch his back," I said. "I

should tell Floss, too, just to be safe."

Knobbe III snorted. "Not just the two of them. Remember the idea of guilt by association. If they get him the way they got him before, you may all go along for the ride."

"How much do you know about what happened before?"

Knobbe III shrugged. "Enough to know that you could all get hurt," he said.

I winced. Guilt by association was a real worry. In our city, just like in the rest of the country, people were being judged more and more by who they knew, rather than by what they did. Knobbe III was right. If Tonio's past caught up with him, if it caused a problem for him now, we could all be in trouble.

I left without buying one single thing.

IX

". . . this forlorn piece of inflammatory speech."

I wandered in the direction of Max and Tonio's, I just didn't wander straight. At one point I noticed that I was walking down Keating, of all streets, and I didn't even blink. Everyone knows that Keating is the place to be if you really want the hard stuff, and the street shows it. Burned-out buildings, vacant lots, and houses that all lean a bit to the east, with high rusty fences and scratchy grass. I walked right down the middle of a sidewalk that was breaking into pieces almost before my eyes, and I skipped all the cracks, but I did it on automatic. Cracks were the last thing on my mind. I must have looked formidable because I didn't get approached by anyone.

I saw a few shapes that moved just out of clear vision range, and I heard police sirens twice, but nothing more than that. I wandered, and I thought, and I wandered some more.

RANDOM THOUGHTS WHILE WANDERING

Knobbe's rumors had to be fallout from Major. I doubted that any outlaw would disagree with me on this. I should tell Tonio what Knobbe knew. Which might make him so angry he'd go after Major in a way that could be detrimental to all concerned.

I should tell Max. But he might just beat Major to the pulpy mass of slime that he was. Nice, but also detrimental.

I should tell Nicholas. In fact, I probably would tell Nicholas. But I didn't see how he'd be any more effective than I was, and even putting us together I didn't see much hope for brilliance.

I should tell Floss. Floss could take us all away. But would she? And if she did, would everyone pick up and leave, or would the Outlaws dissolve?

I should not tell Lucia. Lucia was just starting to feel brave and strong. Lucia was putting computers together and looking happy. I couldn't ruin that, at least not until I knew for sure that it needed to be ruined.

Damned, stupid guilt by association.

When I looked up again I was at Sage and Damen, standing in the shadow of the chocolate factory. I hardly ever noticed the smell now. It was something that seemed like it had always been a part of the Outlaws.

There was a light breeze. One of our banners whispered secrets and dropped them on the sidewalk before I could decode them. I didn't care. At this point any secrets were too much for me. I went home, straight home, and the first person I bumped into when I got there was Floss. This was like having my decision about who to talk to made for me, like the answer to what I should do was written in calligraphic fonts on a little card and delivered on a silver tray.

Floss was wrapped in a Mexican shawl striped in desert paintbrush colors. It couldn't possibly have had even one tiny thing to do with *The Bastard and the Beauty*, so I assumed she just liked it. Liking something Floss liked might be a good way to open up a conversation.

"That's a fine thing," I said. Then I completely ruined my opening ploy by pulling her into the corner of the living room that was the farthest away from any door. This was definitely not slick, and if I'd been trying for subterfuge, this was the worst way to go about it. But I'd never been one for small talk and Floss was even worse. She shook off my hand and glared at me like I'd just said that pink clouds shouldn't have fur trim.

"That's not what you want to say. It couldn't be." Floss folded her arms and waited with raised eyebrows.

I sighed. "No. You're right." And I launched myself into Knobbe III's little story. Getting started felt like jumping off the Keating Street Bridge, the one that I'd crossed not that many minutes before, but once I'd started I couldn't seem to stop. Bridge jumping similarities there, too, I guess. Just plunge on down. I not only told the drink, dust, and magic story, I told all my feelings and all my fears, too. Things I hadn't even known were there. But they certainly were. Whatever calm mellowness Nicholas believed I possessed was simply gone. When I heard what came out of my mouth I realized that I'd been worried since that day when Nicholas came running backstage, giddy about a possible review in *Nighttimes*.

WHAT I SAID TO FLOSS

Drinks, drugs, magic, and pixie dust!

Guilt by association!

Would Tonio get arrested? Again?

If that happened, would Max be able to control himself?

What was going to happen to The Bastard and the Beauty?

Worse, what was going to happen to the Outlaws?

Worse more, what was going to happen to all of us? With Outlaws we were a family. Without it, we were more like a lost bunch of misfits. (Later Floss swore that I wrung my hands at this point, but I think she was just being dramatic.)

Why was this happening? (Said on a long, loud moan.)

During this performance Floss looked angry, disgusted, and finally, sad. Then she said, in a very un-Flosslike way, "If there's fallout from any of this, it's going to hit Tonio, not me, and it could end up being just like before. I can't be part of that. I *won't* be part of that." She added, more to herself than to me, "I'd never put Tonio through that again."

"What does that mean?" It almost sounded like Floss was ready to walk. No more Floss, no more Outlaws. And if she stayed and Tonio was lost? Same thing, really. We were a set, the six of us. Lose one, and everything would start to tumble. I hadn't been wrong when I'd said we were a family. For me, at least, the Outlaws were that proverbial place to come back to, that place where they have to take you in. But even better than that, they were my friends, in the truest sense. I couldn't stand the thought of losing that.

Floss stood there in her corner, wrapped in her rainbow shawl, and finally said, "I wish I had an answer, Persia."

I leaned against the wall, more for support than

for anything else, and stared with care at the space between my feet. I was watching the floor with such intense scrutiny that I didn't know Lucia was there until she spoke.

"Like I said before . . ." It was Lucia's whisper-quiet voice. "We could go to Faerie."

Now it was Floss's turn to slump into the wall. "Doesn't matter," she said, more to herself than to either of us. Then straight to Lucia she said, "That might not be such a good idea." Her voice was the gentle one she used so often with Lucia. "For one thing, there's the troll. You do remember Reginald, right?"

Lucia shivered, but she held firm. "I haven't seen him since forever."

"Maybe not, but if you did, what would you do? When you're with me you've got a modicum of protection. If we go back for an extended stay, I can't promise that I'll always be nearby."

"Maybe he won't have me in his brain anymore. Or maybe he won't recognize me. Didn't you say trolls have bad eyes?"

Floss nodded but said, "They have a terrific sense of smell, though, to make up for the eyes. And they don't forget much of anything."

"Um," I said. "Want to tell me what happened?" It wasn't hard to sound interested, but I didn't want them to think I was chasing a train wreck, either.

"No," Floss said.

"It was a really bad troll," Lucia said. Then she brightened. "But lots of other things are good."

"There's always that dichotomy," Floss said in a cryptic way that sounded more like the usual Floss.

"Oh," I said, because I wasn't sure what else there was to say to that. Instead I asked, "What's the other thing?"

"What?" Floss asked.

"You said for one thing there's a troll. What's the other thing?"

Floss crossed her arms and glared at me.

Lucia's glance moved between Floss and me. She spoke carefully when she said, "Sometimes parts of Floss's family—"

"The ones who rule things?" I asked.

"Right." Lucia cut her eyes toward Floss. "They're—um—they're not necessarily . . ."

She trailed away. Floss sighed and said, "They're hard to deal with."

"Hard to deal with" couldn't be all. I moved my head back and forth between the two of them. Just when I'd decided to ask for more clarification, Nicholas walked through the front door. I don't think he registered the peculiar huddle we were in because the first thing he did was to shoot both arms up in a V-for-Victory gesture and say "Finished! Last final."

We all looked at him. Somehow, in my mind, finals seemed so mundane after Knobbe III's story, after my conversation with Floss, after Lucia and the trolls. But Nicholas was obviously expecting something, so I said, "Congratulations." Even I thought it sounded weak.

He must have really seen the huddle in the corner then because he said, "What's going on?" in a cautious voice, like someone approaching a nervous stray.

I glanced toward the door where Lucia had come out. Was Max back there, ear to the wall? Was Tonio?

At this point, did it even matter? Two-thirds of the Outlaws were here, and most of them already knew what had happened. And maybe, I thought in a sudden burst of optimism, what Knobbe had said about street rumors, the kind that could get us all in trouble, was nothing, after all.

Everyone was looking at me. Too many eyes.

"We should tell him." Lucia was the one who spoke. "We all need to know, after all."

I held on to the optimistic streak that had brushed past me. "You know, maybe it's really nothing. Maybe I—maybe we—overreacted."

Floss snorted. Even Lucia widened her eyes as if to say *You must be kidding me* while Floss added, "Yeah. Right."

Nicholas looked from face to face and finally settled. "Persia?" he asked.

This was when Tonio charged into the room, Max on his heels. Tonio's boots were so loud they were probably knocking plaster off the ceilings of the apartment below.

"Lying little bastard," Tonio muttered. "Damn

him straight to hell on a one-way ticket."

He was holding an official-looking envelope in his hand, one of those big white ones with many markings that always send fear through your heart when they show up in your mail. The envelope fluttered in the breeze Tonio created, flapping its ends like a trapped seagull beating its wings.

Max moved with tiny, quiet steps, not like Max at all. He looked like he was trying to be helpful and solicitous and stay out of the way, all at the same time.

Nicholas watched everything with the attention he'd give a good movie. His eyes got bigger and bigger. Those eyes found me again and once more he said, "Persia?"

"Nicholas," Tonio snapped at exactly the same moment, "you know law. Tell me if this forlorn piece of inflammatory speech says what I think it says." And he thrust the envelope at Nicholas.

Floss was moving closer to Tonio in a slow, steady way. It was as if she were offering moral support by her presence alone. Lucia looked ready to cry. And I just looked from Nicholas to Tonio, from the letter to

Max, from Lucia to Floss.

Nicholas took the envelope and held it between his thumb and forefinger, arm straight out. He seemed dubious.

"Well?" Tonio snapped again. This time he sounded like a quick crack of thunder.

"I haven't read it yet," Nicholas pointed out. "The way everybody's acting, I'm afraid to."

Tonio snapped his eyes. I swear, I almost heard them close and reopen like old wooden shutters. "Read the fucking thing."

Lucia gasped and I coughed. Out of all of us, Tonio was the one who swore the least. Even Lucia beat him.

Tonio grimaced and added, "Please."

Nicholas read. He read for what seemed like a very long time. When he finally looked up he said, "Illegal and magical substances, corrupting minors, and unlawful assembly?"

"Don't ask me. Tell me," Tonio said, harsh voiced.

Nicholas glanced at the paper again, then said, "I could repeat it all without the question mark, but I don't think that's quite what you had in mind." He waved the paper in the air. "What is this?"

"You're supposed to be the law student," Tonio said, but now he didn't sound mad, he just sounded tired. Worn out. And old with it.

"No, I know what it is. It's a subpoena. It's got a court date right here. One week from . . ." He stopped, yanked a phone out of his pocket, clicked through some menus, and nodded. "Yeah, one week from today. But what I meant was, what is this bullshit?"

"Major," Floss said, and I could tell the word was sour in her mouth. "It has to be Major."

"Of course it's Major." Max had been silent for so long that Lucia and I both started when he spoke. "I just don't know how he found someone gullible enough to go along with this."

"The word's out on the street." My voice sounded flat and dull. "Pink drinks, and red ones too. Pixie dust. Magical potions on top of magic, all courtesy of the Outlaws. Knobbe Three said. And he always knows. All Major really needed were a few of the right shills to start spreading the word."

After a couple of beats of silence Floss said, "Apparently he found them."

Nicholas said, in a very careful voice, "At least the drinks were pink and red. Now, if they'd been touted as purple . . ."

We all stared at him until I finally said, "What?"

"You know. The darker the color, the more illegal the substance." He lifted his eyebrows and looked hopeful. When no one responded he sighed. "It was supposed to sort of be a joke?"

I patted his hand. "Sure. Obviously."

Tonio sat down in the middle of the room. Crumbled down, actually, with none of his usual grace. His voice was painful to hear when he said, "I can't do this again. I thought I could, but I can't." He looked way, way up at Max. "Don't let this happen to me. Please."

I thought my heart would break. If it did, it would be so loud that everyone in the room would hear it.

Lucia had the tears that I wanted to cry running down her face. "Don't go," she whispered. She waved at the paper that Nicholas still held. He looked like he was holding a rotting fish by the tail. "Just don't show up," Lucia continued. She sat next to Tonio and took his hand. "We'll hide."

I looked at everything crammed into Max's apartment. I thought of all we'd left behind at the chocolate factory. I thought, too, of all of us, and I asked, "Where? How? Because if he can't get Tonio, you can bet he'll go for Max. And if he can't get Max, he'll go for one of us."

"We didn't do anything," Lucia wailed, and she cried even harder. Tonio put his arm around her shoulders and she buried her face in his collar.

"When this happened before," Nicholas said. "Um, I mean—well, what did happen? With the prison sentence and all." He sounded like his question might be in bad taste, but that it needed to be asked anyway.

"Furies of badness akin to the Dark Courts of Evil," muttered Floss.

It was all too much for me—the tension, the thick hard air, the innuendos. I lost all the calm that I was supposed to possess. "Floss," I snapped, "what the hell are you talking about? Speak English, for Mab's sake."

"If I'm speaking for Mab's sake, I don't need to

worry about what you do and don't understand, mortal." Her eyes actually flashed and she moved a step closer to me.

I didn't know this Floss. I stepped back, moving fast, and tripped on Tonio. I would have landed flat on the floor if Max hadn't grabbed me and kept me upright.

"Enough," Max said. His tone was hard and strong and fierce. "Enough, all of you. Just stop everything for one minute. None of you are helping him"—he pointed, of course at Tonio—"and all of you are hurting one another. I don't have the resources to keep anyone else upright and functioning right now. We all have to take care of one another if we're going to come out of this intact. But I have to say that right now, Tonio is my main concern."

He glared at each of us in turn, then added, "Am I making all this clear?"

Nicholas was the first to speak. "He's right. We can't help if we spend all our energy infighting."

"Sorry," Floss said, staring at the floor between my feet.

"Sorry, too," I said. I looked straight at Floss when I spoke, willing her to look up. When I saw her eyelids flicker, I added, "Sorrier, actually. I spoke first."

Floss shrugged, but she lifted her head. She looked like Floss again.

Lucia was still next to Tonio. She said, "Nicholas is right. Max, too. We have to work with one another. It's important." She sounded so sincere, so honest, that I almost smiled. If we couldn't get together behind Lucia, who could we get behind?

And just like that, snap, we were the Outlaws again. Now in more ways than one, apparently, because with the mess we were in, who knew what we might have to do next?

X

"The answer's in the petals."

$\mathscr{N}$icholas was buried in precedents. He wasn't finding much, or so it seemed, because he kept growling and smacking books on the table. Every time he did that Floss, who was sitting across from him folding complicated-looking paper flowers, would jump and swear in a soft, controlled, not-at-all-like-Floss way.

Max and Tonio were sitting close, talking in low inaudible voices. Lucia was in the kitchen boiling water for gallons of tea. And me? I was drifting, on the move because I couldn't seem to sit still. Really, at this point in time, book art didn't seem to be what was called for, and I wasn't sure what else to offer.

"Persia," Floss said. I thought she was irritated because I kept wandering back and forth behind her chair, but all she seemed to want was help. "Come here. These still need stems."

"Okay." If I couldn't do books, I could still do paper.

Floss rolled a stem, slim and perfect. It looked like she was rolling an exquisite joint. I tried one and it looked more like an unwieldy cigar. "Hmmm," I said. Making flower stems was more difficult than making a book with cross bindings. I held my stem up for a Floss inspection. She barely glanced at it, then said, in an unusually calm tone, "That's fine."

"So, Floss," I said to keep my mind as occupied as my fingers. "Why are we making flowers?"

She looked at me sideways and sighed. If she'd said, "Stupid question," she wouldn't have been any clearer. But all she really did say was, "I need to get a message home and I don't have time to go myself."

I rolled a few more stems while I thought about this. My stems were getting better, which was probably the only nice thing that had happened today, but I still couldn't make the connection between Floss's words and what my hands were doing. "I don't get it," I admitted, after a full minute of thinking.

Floss pursed her lips. She grabbed a small clay pot and smacked it down between us, smacked it hard enough that Nicholas looked up briefly and frowned. Floss ignored him and dumped a bunch of stemmed flowers in the pot. Like magic they rearranged themselves, became a lively little bouquet. She added three of the flowers with my stems. They sprang to life too, although I could tell that the weight of the stems was dragging them down.

Floss waved her hands over the pot and the new green smell of spring filled the room. Even Tonio and Max looked our way. Then Floss leaned in close to the flowers and whispered. They nodded their little flower heads, just once, so fast that I almost doubted what I'd seen.

"Now," Floss said, "I put them on the back porch, near the steps. Then a flyer picks up the message, delivers it, and brings the answer back."

"How do you know when the answer's here?" I was amazed by all of this. Fey air mail. "Does someone show up at the door or what?"

Floss raised her eyes to the ceiling and sighed. "No, Persia. The flowers die. The answer's in the petals." And she waved her hands over the flowers again. The life washed out of the vibrant petals, and a few small pieces of paper fell to the table, touching the wood with a whisper of sound. I looked at them, looked hard, but there were no words, no symbols that I could see, nothing at all.

I pointed. "Is that it? The answer?"

Floss sighed again. "Were these by the back door?" She raised both eyebrows before she added, "Think before you speak."

Oh.

"A demonstration, right?"

Floss nodded.

"How did you . . ." I touched one paper petal and heard it rasp against my finger.

Floss shrugged, waved the flowers back to life, said, "Magic," and went back to rolling the last few stems.

Lucia came in just as the flowers sprang to life for

the second time. She carried a teapot the size of a small porcupine, which she set carefully in the middle of the table. She sniffed the green spring in the air and watched the flowers nod in a breeze I couldn't feel, then said, "You're sending a message. What does it say?"

Floss looked straight up at Lucia and said, "What we need for Tonio. Help."

The flowers were dead before dusk. Lucia found them when she took the tea leaves out to the compost bucket. She called Floss, her voice pitched high with something that was either excitement or nerves.

I followed Floss out to the tiny porch above the back stairs. Paper petals were scattered across the scarred peeling wood like rune stones. Floss scanned the porch from right to left, from left to right, then trudged inside, head down.

Trudged. Floss didn't trudge, she always moved with the grace of a trained ballet dancer.

I swallowed and licked my lips. "Lucia?"

When she turned to look at me she moved as if

her eyes were being pulled away from those petals by a slow puppet string. When I saw those eyes my stomach dipped.

"It's bad, isn't it?" I asked.

Lucia took a long breath. "I don't read flowers very well," she hedged, but when a tear dribbled down her cheek I didn't really believe her.

"Floss didn't look too happy," I pointed out, "so it must not be good."

She stared at me and said, "Well." The word seemed to be dragged out of her throat. It was followed, with equal slowness, by "I think it says they won't help."

As if further explanation was needed, she kept talking in that same sad little voice. "She's always been the odd one. In her family most of them practically glow with fey righteousness. In Faerie, that righteousness is intense. There's not a lot of room for those who don't follow the prescribed line. It all makes Floss stand out. Her younger brother's the only one who's like her, and he hides it much better." Lucia stopped for a second and smiled a wistful, secret little smile; then she continued. "And she spends all this time here with us. She doesn't go home much at all. And if she does, she doesn't see them. So I think—I guess they don't see much point in helping her now."

I absorbed this Floss information. It was nothing like what I'd expected to hear. Not the part about no help. I'd pretty much gotten that already. But the family part. That was what I hadn't understood before when Floss said her family was hard to deal with. I understood it now. It sounded like I'd left home for almost the same reasons that Floss didn't go home. For my part, I couldn't stomach the conservative, holier-than-thou attitudes that were supposed to be my life guidelines, especially when they came from my drugged-out, fey-phobic parents. I wondered just what ideas Floss and her parents differed on, but I didn't bother to ask. I didn't think I'd get an answer. It seemed, though, that Floss and I had a lot more in common than I'd ever thought. Neither of us did what we were supposed to do, and neither of us, apparently, were big on family bonding.

Still, Floss and Faerie had been our golden door,

our last-ditch escape route, at least in my mind. If things were as bad as Lucia said, I was afraid that we were in big trouble.

I made a sharp right turn and marched back inside. I passed Nicholas, who was putting more water on to boil. He looked at me, looked behind me at Lucia, set the kettle in the sink with barely a sound, and followed us without saying one word.

Our little parade stepped in time past Tonio and Max, who were still huddled. It seemed like they'd been that way talking, talking for days. Even they noticed that something was happening. They fell in behind Nicholas, which meant that all the Outlaws were together when I went up to Floss. She was sitting in her workroom, hands oddly still, and she seemed to look deep into an emptiness I couldn't see. I hated to disturb that contemplation, but we needed to know what we had for options. That date on Tonio's subpoena was getting closer hour by hour.

"Lucia says it's bad news," I blurted. "She says they won't help."

Floss focused on me, then her eyes widened as she

saw everyone behind me, but all she said was, "My, word travels so quickly here." Her tone was very mild.

I know I slumped. I'd really wanted Lucia to be wrong. I'd really wanted to know we had some excellent, last-minute place we could go to if it came to that. In fact, I'd counted on it all along. Whenever something seemed to be getting worse I'd think, well, we can always run to Faerie. Lucia did it when she needed a place to hide. We could do it too. Except now it looked like we couldn't. Or if we did, it might not be much better than here, at least for Floss. Same problem, different players, sort of.

Floss let her eyes scan each of us; then she said, "My family members aren't the only inhabitants of Faerie, you know."

"It's true," Lucia said. "But you do have to know that some of the other ones can be scary." As an afterthought she added, "At least sometimes."

I remembered Lucia and Floss's earlier conversation about the troll. I started to ask about him again, but I saw Floss's lips curve into an almost smile, so I waited. "As you say," she said to Lucia. "But, as you've also said, just some of them and even those aren't always frightening. Some of the scary things you're remembering are probably mind leftovers from when you first crossed over. You were alone then. Everything's scarier when you're alone."

In an even voice Lucia said, "That's true. And I know about the good ones too. There's El Jeffery, for sure. And Freddy." When she said the name Freddy her voice became gentle and her eyes shone. Then she stood a little straighter and added, "But even though I think we need to keep Faerie as an option, I want them to know everything's not perfect. That's important. For decision making."

I wanted to know who the people Lucia mentioned were. Was El Jeffery Floss's brother? Was Freddy an old friend? I wanted to know just what we'd meet in Faerie, if we ever did go. I didn't ask because Floss nodded her head and, as this was a conversation about her home, I figured whatever she said took precedence. What she said was, "Of course, and you're right. They need to be prepared if and when they do go. But remember, when you're with me now we move quickly. We're on a mission of some type. Scouting locations. Looking for silver down. Things like that. We don't really chat much with most beings. We really don't even see many people. Scariness has different levels."

"We should at least mention the ones I see out of the corners of my eyes sometimes," Lucia said, sounding firm. "Those are the ones I think they need to know about the most."

Floss shrugged. It made her look like the Floss I was used to, and it was reassuring. "If they're eye-corner creatures, of course they're scary," Floss said. "That's their job, after all."

I filed that bit of information away, just in case.

Floss was still talking. "But there are people I'm on good terms with. Lots of them. So don't despair. At least not about that, not yet. Just keep what Lucia said in mind. She's right in thinking that it could influence your decision."

Tonio spoke out loud for the first time in what seemed like months. "I agree with Floss. We have so many more things we can despair about just now."

I twisted around to see him, because if Floss sounded like Floss, Tonio sounded even more like Tonio. His eyes had a little of their spark back and he looked taller and stronger. I wondered, not for the first time, just what he and Max had been saying to each other during all those long hours of huddled discussion.

Tonio kept talking. "Let's all just despair about getting through today. And then tomorrow. Something's bound to happen soon."

Max put his hand on Tonio's shoulder. They looked so strong, so together, that I tried to let myself relax for the first time since we'd gotten Major's message. And it worked, for right then. But it was hard to keep the tension at bay. For me the feelings just snuck up every now and then, like the little nudges a kitten makes when it rubs its head on your ankle, or nips at your fingertips. And as time wandered on I could tell by the way different people acted that our problems had to be tugging on their minds too.

So what do people do when they're in a tense, tight situation? The kind that sometimes makes breathing hard, that wakes you up in the middle of the night and makes you rub your stomach, that peers over your shoulder and occasionally bumps into you just so you don't forget it's there?

Here's what the Outlaws did. We performed, adhering to that old adage, "The show must go on." And we performed to large crowds. The street talk didn't seem to keep anyone away. In fact, it almost seemed to play in our favor. Kind of like saying, "We know some of the weeds in the abandoned lots are drugs. Make sure you report it if you find it." Which of course makes everyone start looking in every abandoned lot they can find and makes no one start reporting a thing. So sure, some people came looking for drugs, but even if they did, when they didn't find any they still stayed. And the rest? They came to see a great show, which is exactly what they got. The power of the Outlaws!

We played to sold-out houses, and we played well. As Tonio's court date came closer we played with a kind of desperation. It was almost as if we believed that good shows would keep the demons, and the law, away from us. And it worked, sort of. Floss swore she didn't see even one demon of any kind, and no police ever showed up to challenge an audience.

There was one afternoon when Floss stopped in the middle of painting eye makeup on a flying fish and simply stood in place, brush in hand. I was walking past, arms filled with that night's programs, and noticed the lack of normal Floss frenzy. I never knew if Floss was simply hyper or if being fey gave her extra energy, but she was always doing *something*. It was as if her fingers and her brain had to be active for her to be happy. I said, "Something wrong?"

Floss shook her head like a wet dog. Then she focused on me. "Persia," she said.

"Right. Many points scored." I watched her, waiting.

"That was so strange," she said, more to herself than to me. "You didn't feel that, did you?"

"Since I don't know what you're talking about, probably no," I said.

"Huh," Floss said. "Oh, well."

When she didn't say anything more I asked, "And the thing I was supposed to feel?"

Floss shrugged. "It felt like a presence from Faerie just walked through the room. Or passed by outside. Somewhere close to us, at least. It was dim, almost as if it was wearing a mask, but it definitely felt fey."

"Floss," I said carefully, "I don't think I'm your best bet to spy masked fey presences."

She shrugged again. "Why not?"

I narrowed my eyes. "Maybe you have me confused with Lucia?"

"Of course not." Floss waved her hand in a dismissive gesture and black paint floated off her brush and landed on the floor in a kanji design. "You're as sensitive as anyone else."

This was news to me, but before I could question her, Floss said, "If it *was* fey and it *was* masked it could be for any number of reasons. People come and go on a regular basis, and not all of them want to be seen. Or felt, if it comes to that." She twisted her fish and looked at the other eye. "I've noticed things like this before," she added. "Nothing comes of it . . . usually."

Usually. Not reassuring. But maybe I was just being paranoid. Still. "Usually?" I repeated.

Floss brushed the koi's eye with shadow, then held the fish up for inspection. I walked behind her and stared at it, nose to nose. "Beautiful," I said. "And—usually?"

She shook her head. "Persia, we've got so many things to worry about right now. Let's not add something that has a high probability of being nothing."

And because she was Floss, and she knew about fey, I decided to go along with her. Because, after all, if she'd felt this before and there hadn't been any repercussions, why worry now? As Floss said, we had enough other things to deal with.

One of those things was that there was more and more street news about dust and drinks. There still weren't any that we knew of at our performances, though, and if there were, we knew for certain that we weren't supplying. We shoved that news off into the corner too, the corner occupied by the unnamed fey presence.

As far as we could tell, there wasn't a connection between any of this—masked presences, dust, or drinks—and Tonio and the subpoena. It caused me to breathe deep when I realized that fact, and it felt like the first calm, deep breath I'd taken since I last talked to Knobbe III. Then I remembered our legal issues and I went back to little, shallow breaths, the kind that never seemed to get enough air into my lungs.

The one good thing that happened was actually a nonevent. None of us saw Major at all.

The court date, though? That still kept coming, stalking toward us like Lucia in her chicken suit. Big slapping steps, loud and forceful.

Nicholas pulled me aside one afternoon and said, "Persia, I'm getting desperate. I've looked through every damn thing I can find and I can't see any way to keep Tonio from having to go to court. I was sure I'd find some neat, tricky little loophole, but right now this seems so tight. I don't know what to do next."

I put on my happy face, just like donning a mask, and said, "They can't really prove anything, can they? It's all so nebulous, isn't it? It'll turn out okay, won't—"

Nicholas stopped my babbling questions by saying, "What the hell are you talking about? Of course they can prove something. Even if it's not true, I'm pretty sure Major's got all his witnesses lined up and ready to go."

"But if they lie, that's perjury, isn't it? That's unlawful too, right? I mean——"

"Persia." He sounded desperate. "Stop talking in questions. And think before you open your mouth."

Third time in recent history that I'd been told that. It was sort of cosmic, really.

"But Nicholas——"

"No. Stop. Here's what you need to do. Go see Knobbe Three. Get his take on the news on the street."

I started to say something, but he shook his head and just kept talking. "I know you already talked to him. Do it again. He knows everything. See if there have been any changes."

When I still stood there, not moving, he reached out and caught my hand in his. "Please, Persia? I need help. I feel like everyone's waiting for me to pull something magic out of the air, and I can't. I'm not Floss. I'm not even Lucia. I'm a dumb student. I'm trying to apply everything I've learned, and none of it's working."

I wrapped my other hand around his, a three-hand clasp. "You're not dumb" was the first thing out of my mouth.

Nicholas almost laughed. "I wasn't compliment fishing."

"I know. It's just important that you know that."

He cleared his throat, but I didn't wait for him to talk. "I'll go see Knobbe Three," I said, and I walked out the door.

XI

"A little something for the road."

"Hello, Knobbe Three," I said. I was quiet, walking on pins, talking in whispers.

Knobbe III nodded and his eyes traveled through the store. It was crowded, people hunched in all the little nooks and crannies. I wasn't comfortable asking questions, not with all those ears around.

I said, "Big run on stationery today?" which made him grin.

"Letter Writers Anonymous conference in town," he said, and he smiled again.

"What a good thing I bought my calling cards last week."

Three people came up to the counter. In quick

succession Knobbe sold one journal, four sheets of gold wrapping paper trimmed with green baby rabbits, two calligraphy pens, a set of paper and envelopes in pumpkin orange, and a rubber stamp that looked like it said, "Eyes are for lying." I stood off to one side and I waited.

When the foot traffic had cleared I said, "So, what's the word on the street?"

"Depends on which word you're looking for."

"*The Bastard and the Beauty*?" I prompted.

Knobbe III stopped smiling. "How's the box office doing?"

"Fine." I was cautious.

"It's possible that may not continue."

"Very oblique, Knobbe."

He shrugged. "No. Not really. Word on the street isn't all that great. And it's got nothing to do with the actuality of *The Bastard and the Beauty*."

I tried not to bite my lip. "Is it worse than it was the last time we talked?"

A little struggle walked across his face before he said, "Only the illegal substances part. The magic stories are still there, but they don't seem to be escalating. Those colored drinks and pixie dust, though—people seem to love those. I saw some graffiti just yesterday. 'Get high free at B&B.'"

I said, "Grr," which made him nod.

"Some of the drinks are turning purple now, and blue. Just to—you know—liven things up."

Purple and blue. Like Nicholas had said, everyone knew that the tougher the drug the deeper the color. Pink was bad enough to get a subpoena. Red was nastier, but still on the top, the safer end of the spectrum. Purple and blue, though—those colors would make it that much easier to make a case.

All of this must have been plain to read on my face, because Knobbe held out his hand, an imprinted button nestled in his palm. "A little something for the road."

I picked up the smooth white button. I read the etched black word on its face and I smiled. "Outlaws?" Then Knobbe's words caught up with me. "For the road?"

"You never know. And we're all on a road to somewhere."

"I suppose that's a certainty," I muttered.

I pinned the button to my shirt, making sure it was directly over my heart. Then I reached out and brushed my fingertips against his. "Thanks, Knobbe Three," I said, and I went back out onto the street.

Nicholas was sitting on the thick, concrete steps when I got back, framed by the porch railings and the front door lintel. Casual as a Saturday afternoon, at least at first glance. At second glance he was a lot more like rush hour on a Monday morning. When he saw me coming down the street he sat up straight and looked anxiously hopeful. I tried to look the same way, but I think he carried it off much better than I.

I got close enough that he could read my button. "Outlaws?" he asked.

"It's a present. From Knobbe."

"Depending on interpretation, that could be nice."

"Yeah, depending. He says it's for the road." I sat down next to him.

Nicholas dropped his head. If I'd been behind him, it would have looked like he'd been cut off at

130

the neck. "That bad, huh?" He breathed out hard and looked at me sideways. "Crap, Persia. What are we going to do?"

I bounced a little on my step, agitated. "You're asking me? Why don't you ask someone who might know? Floss. Or Max. You'd probably get a better answer out of Lucia, even."

He looked at me then, looked for what seemed like a long time, and then said, "No, I wouldn't. It's pretty much you and me right now. Floss is upset about that message she got from Faerie. Lucia's trying to be strong, but you know how she can flip to fragile. Max is all wrapped up in Tonio, and Tonio's either just fine or having a nice, quiet nervous breakdown. I never know which. We've got a subpoena saying we're passing out drugs in public places and using magic on top of that.

"As long as we're at the theater, we're fine. There we can take anything in stride. Take us out of that environment and we fall apart." He sighed and, trying to sound movie-star tough, repeated, "It's you and me, kid." And he grinned a sad, weak little grin.

"Nicholas, I'm not good at stuff like this."

He stood up. He stared down. Way down. Why hadn't I realized how tall he was? After all, I'd known him a long time. He said, "You'd better get good at it, then. Fast. I need help. You and I are what we've got."

I stood up too, right next to him, on the same step. Not so tall after all. "I think it needs to be a group effort. Right now that's my best contribution. We need to plan, and the hell with all the problems. And the hell with them expecting you to save us. That's not fair, not any more fair than you expecting me to know the answer."

I took his hand and pulled. "Let's go inside and get this thing started."

Nicholas huffed out a little laugh. "See? I knew I picked the right person." And he squeezed my hand.

I just tugged a little harder. We walked into the apartment, our hands still pressed tight together. In spite of everything, that warmth of his palm against mine felt very good.

I could see right away that Nicholas had given me a good synopsis of the situation. We didn't even look like a group at this point. More like random people you'd run across in a park or, worse, in a bus station waiting room. Everyone was scattered, each wrapped in his or her own thoughts, each staked out in different areas of different rooms.

"Oh," I said.

Nicholas breathed out a little puff of air and said, "Yeah."

Someone had to do something or we'd drift apart like Floss's paper flowers. I glanced at Nicholas, who shook his head and shrugged.

I squared my shoulders and took one deep breath. "All right," I said, loud enough that they could hear me no matter where they were. "I've made a decision."

No one even looked our way.

"I knew you'd be excited," I said. "And here it is. No more negative thoughts."

Heads came up and eyes looked at me—flat, dull eyes. Then they turned back to the fascinating floors or tables in front of them. It didn't look like peppy talk was the right approach.

I picked the least sad-looking person in the

apartment. "Lucia," I said, "what do you think we need to do?"

Her eyes went straight to mine, almost as if she'd been waiting for a chance to tell us her plan. "Go to work. Do a great show. Then leave."

From the other side of the room Floss coughed. "And go where?"

"Faerie," Lucia said. There was no room for discussion in her calm, one-word statement.

"You know—," Floss began, but Lucia cut her off. Surprises every day.

"So they said no. So you're sad. You probably feel betrayed. But this is more important than that. We need to help Tonio. And going is all I can think of. We'll find a way to make things work when we get there. It's not easy when you've been hurt," Lucia finished in a new, quiet voice, "but you can do it."

"Scary corner-of-the-eye creatures," Floss said. "Remember? And Reginald?"

Lucia breathed deep and said, "If we're together, things will be fine." She nodded, then added, "It's being together that's important."

I looked at Lucia with respect. She was right, and she'd been so clear. Not my "no negative thoughts," not Nicholas's precedents, not Floss's flower messages. Lucia had just made a plain, straight decision. And then Max stood up, tall and strong, and he said, "Yes. Absolutely right. It's being together." He smiled—a small smile but a better smile than I'd seen since this mess started. "Let's go to work, let's knock them out of their seats, let's disappear." He looked at Tonio. "Very Outlawish. I like this plan."

Tonio sighed, long and low, then said, "Oh, what the hell. We haven't got anything better." He looked around the apartment. "Although I hate to leave everything . . ." His voice trailed off.

"It's not forever," Max said.

"We'll come back," Lucia promised.

"It might be good, just for a while," I added. "Knobbe Three says things are just going to get worse. And you really don't want to keep that court date."

"I'll go," Nicholas said, on a rush of air. "I've always wanted to go, I just never knew how. But if Floss can take us . . ."

"I'm not a tour guide," Floss snapped. "There's not a Lonely Planet for Faerie."

"But you could take us, right? You know how."

"It's not a question of how," Floss said to him. "I obviously know how. Lucia and I go, remember? And you could get there on your own as long as your need was strong enough."

"I've tried," Nicholas mumbled. "I've thought, and I've wished, and all I've ever gotten is me, standing under an oak, looking like a fool."

"Really?" I asked. "I never knew . . ."

"Enough want but not enough need," Floss snapped again, interrupting me. Even though she sounded dismissive, I was sure that was only because she was upset. She proved that when she said, "You're all acting like this is a lark, a little trip to the circus. I know it, and it's not what you think. The possibility for danger is always there."

"Right now that's a good, strong possibility for here," Nicholas pointed out, apparently taking no offense at Floss's statement about want and need. Then he nodded at Tonio and said, "At least for him it is. Jail's no picnic."

Max said, flat and true, "No shit."

"Floss," I said, "you said it yourself, before, and you were right. Tonio can't go to prison. We all agree on that. I know I couldn't do it once, let alone twice. We have to do something."

"Major," Floss said, and it was easy to see how bad the word tasted in her mouth. "Major or Faerie? That's it?"

"They may not convict him," Nicholas said, almost as if he was changing the subject. "We may be worrying for nothing. We can take the chance." He shrugged. "I'm not feeling too confident about that, but maybe everyone else is and I don't know it."

"Not me," I said.

Lucia shook her head. Max and Tonio just looked at Floss, and I think it was that look that did it, that Floss–Tonio connection. She dropped her head, she dropped her attitude, and she said, soft as spring rain, "All right. All right. I'll come up with something to make this work."

XII

"Tiny street theater!"

*W*e took Lucia's advice. We trooped off to the chocolate factory, and I tried not to think about anything but *The Bastard and the Beauty*. I was doing so well, too, until just before curtain time. That was when Tonio came backstage and said, "There are a lot of empty seats out there."

Max jerked up his head. "We sold a full house."

"Looks like the street talk finally caught up with us. Knobbe Three was right after all," Tonio said, looking at me.

I sighed. "He so often is. It's really tiresome."

Tonio managed a smile. The rest of us stood in a huddle until Max said, "Okay, boys and girls, time to play."

We seemed to inhale once, in sync, and the show began.

It was a good show, one of our best. The connection between the Outlaws and the audience was like a fine, bright wire that stretched between us, a tightrope that words and magic walked on all night long.

"Swan song," Nicholas muttered between acts, but he didn't seem unhappy. In fact, none of us did. We were buoyant, like nothing could touch us, high as the proverbial kite.

But of course the kite comes down sometime. It's the laws of physics, and of gravity. After the curtain call Floss said, "He's out there. Major. Standing by the entrance looking pleased. Looking proud." She frowned. "There's a travel look about him too."

"What's a 'travel look'?" I asked.

Floss shook her head. She seemed frustrated. "I can't explain it better than that. There's just an aura about him that says he's been someplace recently. Someplace far from here."

"Alabama?" I suggested.

"Greece?" Lucia asked.

"I don't know," Floss said. "It's almost like he's masked it, but I doubt he'd know how." She stopped talking and glanced at Lucia and me. "Alabama or Greece?" she asked, and she sounded incredulous.

"Bastard," Nicholas said, before we could answer. There was no emotion at all in his voice. I knew "bastard" wasn't a place, or any kind of a reference to Lucia or to me. I was sure this lack of emotion was because, if he'd let himself feel, he would have turned physical. At least, that was the way my mind was working. I wanted to punch something. Hard. Rabbit punches like I'd seen Max use in training.

Max poked his head around the curtain and pulled it back fast. He shook his head and said, "It's that supercilious smile he wears that irritates me more than anything."

There was silence. There were eyes moving back and forth. Then, suddenly, there was Floss. "This is no fun," she enunciated carefully. "I believe we have a plan that needs to be executed. I suggest we start it now."

She turned and walked toward the back door, the one that led to the alley. Lucia watched her, then said, "We should follow her." She nodded. "Everybody, we should follow Floss."

And like a mandate had been issued, that's just what we did. As we got close to the door, Floss made some complicated movements with her left wrist and, as if it had been there all along, hidden by a thin glamour, a door opened in the door. A scent of rainbows and blood wafted in. We stepped through, and that was how the Outlaws, in a chicken suit, tuxedo, and dinner dress, among other articles of clothing, ended up in Faerie.

FIRST IMPRESSIONS OF FAERIE

Bright, bright colors.

Smells of flowers and sunshine, rain and death.

Excellent grass, soft winds.

Feelings of lightness, as if all my burdens were gone.

The smacking sound of the door of the chocolate factory closing us in, closing our world out.

Very large creature approaching from the right.

"Floss." I wanted to sound calm, but my voice came out more like a baby-doll squeak as I pointed to the mass of feathers and fur that was moving toward us. Whatever the creature was, with its hawklike face, its wings, and its huge lion paws, I was sure I should be standing behind someone who knew what was what, not facing it on my own. Floss turned. She smiled the first real smile I'd seen from her in days. "Ohhh," she whispered, and then she ran and flung herself into the thing's furry arms.

I moved very carefully and stopped near Lucia. In a low voice I said, "Is this one of those corner-of-the-eye things? One of those scary things that sneaks up on you?"

Lucia was smiling too, just like Floss. Not cringing, not hiding, not acting at all like this was a scary thing. She yanked off her chicken feet and her chicken hat and said, "Persia! Of course not. It's El Jeffery," as if that explained everything. And she hurried toward the creature and Floss. The next thing I knew, she was wrapped in a group hug that obviously had nothing to do with trolls, blood, or holes in bridges.

I'd already learned something, or at least I thought I had. It seemed obvious that El Jeffery, one of the names Lucia had mentioned in our old life, couldn't be Floss's brother, unless family relationships in Faerie were amazingly strange.

I fidgeted, not sure where to turn or what to do next. I glanced at the other Outlaws. Nicholas was looking around with a smile on his face that said Christmas. Tonio looked more relaxed than I'd seen him since Major, and Max looked wary.

It seemed to take forever for Floss and Lucia to break away. When they did Floss said, "This is El Jeffery," to us, and to El Jeffery she said, "And these are my friends." She sounded proud of us, Outlaws and creature alike. Lucia stood to one side, her hands wrapped around one of El Jeffery's thick lion-like paws.

"El Jeffery and I grew up together," Floss continued. "We've been like this forever." She held up two fingers, crossed.

El Jeffery laughed, a warm, thick sound. Blackberry wine or blueberry syrup. That laugh poured over me and I sighed happily. I felt the same way that Tonio seemed to feel, like I was back on smooth ground after miles of walking through fields of land mines. Then he or she started coming toward us.

I couldn't help it. I started backing up. So big, and so . . .

"There's nothing to fear. I could never harm a friend of Floss's."

Floss smacked El Jeffery on the forearm, still smiling. "You couldn't harm anyone. Don't pretend to be fierce for effect."

"Band name," El Jeffery said immediately, and if a feathered face could grin, that's what happened.

"Fierce for Effect." Lucia squinted her eyes as if she were looking at the name in lights and then nodded. "It's not bad."

Floss raised her eyebrows. "Flailing Nails was better."

"More punk, though," El Jeffery said. "Doesn't match your guitar style."

"Wait! Floss plays guitar?" I asked.

El Jeffery looked surprised. "She never told you?"

"He exaggerates," Floss said. "He always makes it sound like I know what I'm doing."

"It's way better than my tambourines and jangles," said Lucia.

"You play tambourine?" I asked. And what was a jangle? How could I know so little about the people I thought I knew?

Nicholas spun in place, still looking dazed and pleased. "I feel like I'm five years old." Then he stopped spinning, looked straight at Floss, and said, "Why did you keep this a secret for so long?"

"I didn't. It was always here. It's not my fault you couldn't find it."

"Right," he agreed. "Want and need." His grin stretched wide and he spun again. "This is just so great!"

"Don't forget," Lucia cautioned, "it's not always quite as great as it seems."

"Nothing ever is," Tonio said. "That's why so much of what we do is doomed to fail." His expression didn't match his words. He still looked calm and peaceful.

"Cheery," said Max, but I noticed that he and Tonio

were holding hands like they meant it, something I hadn't seen for a very long time. That in itself seemed to make this a worthwhile venture.

So there we all were in Faerie. There were little hills rolling away to my right. The grass underfoot was soft and springy and looked nothing like the grass I would have seen at home. Even the sun seemed brighter and, at the same time, more benevolent. There wasn't a drop of blood in sight. Major was trapped on the other side of a magic door. Everything seemed practically perfect.

Maybe we could make a play out of all this badness we'd been dealing with. "The Outlaws' Escape," I said, giving the words shiny, capital letters.

"Huh?" said Nicholas elegantly.

"A new play," I said. "We——"

"We all play ourselves," Lucia cried.

"What," Floss said, "is the fun in that?"

"Right." That was Tonio. "The whole point of us is puppets."

"And magic," said Floss.

"And commentary," said Max.

I said, "But it's the story line. We do play us; we just sex it up with the puppets and Floss's wonders."

"Sex it up?" Nicholas asked.

I blushed, but I still said yes to Nicholas and pretended to ignore Tonio's laughter, which he tried to cover up by coughing and saying, "It might be a little ambitious. After all, we don't really know how it ends."

"Ah, but does anything ever really end?"

Floss snorted. "Max, you sound like Derrida or Nietzsche."

"Or Shakespeare." Tonio punched him on the arm. "But seriously, I think we need time to adjust. If we're going to play here—in both senses of the word—I think we need to start small."

"I know," Lucia cried. "I know just what we need to do!"

El Jeffery patted her head with one of his lion paws and looked at the rest of us with round, green eyes. "Lucia has good ideas. You should listen to her."

Lucia grinned up at him as if she'd been given star XM390 for a birthday present and said, "Bicycle theater!"

There was silence. Then everyone looked at her, and El Jeffery said, "Let me rephrase that. Lucia often has good ideas." He paused. Then "Lucia sometimes has good ideas. Or—may have good ideas."

He might have kept talking, but now it was Lucia's turn to punch something. She chose El Jeffery's arm. I'd never once seen Lucia punch someone, seriously or in play. Lucia in Faerie and Lucia at home seemed to be two very different people.

"This is a great idea," she said. "Like Tonio said, it gives us a chance to adapt. It gives us time to relax and scope out the lay of the land. It keeps us busy, but it's not taxing." She beamed.

That silence again until I said, "Um, Lucia, what is bicycle theater?"

She seemed shocked when she said, "You don't know?" Multiple heads shook back and forth in the universal gesture for no.

"Oh. Well . . ." Lucia seemed at a loss for words. "I thought everyone . . ." She trailed off again.

"Lucia, I don't think so," said Nicholas, while Floss watched her with wide, encouraging eyes.

Lucia pulled herself together, a visible movement, took a deep breath, and said, "Bicycle theater. Okay. You set up a traveling stage. A small one. You can mount it on a trailer or on the bicycle itself. Then you do your show wherever, whenever, with little puppets. And you have a coin box so people can drop in money for the show. And music too, if you want. Or little lights. Or—"

"Tiny street theater!" Tonio crowed. "Taking Outlaws back to its roots."

"In a small way," Max said. "Pun intended."

"Multiple setups. We could go all over." Nicholas looked at the land, the hills, the dirt paths, the rocks in the road and added, "You can ride a bicycle around here, can't you, Floss?"

"Depending on where you want to go," she said in that oblique Floss way.

"In town." That was El Jeffery. "It could work in town, or near Dau Hermanos."

"Uh, Floss?" I said. "Isn't there something about the fey and metal? Bikes are metal, right? Do they even have metal things here? Because going back to get a bike or a couple of bikes might—"

Floss coughed to stop me and said, "Titanium."

"What?"

"Steel is horrible stuff. Everybody knows. Titanium, though, that's just fine. Plus it shimmers like a rainbow when it's in the sun. Especially," she said after a moment of contemplation, "if it's purple."

There was really only one answer to that. "Oh," I said, and Floss nodded once, very regally.

El Jeffery said, "You have those bikes in the shed, you know," and I saw Floss stiffen. It was so slight a movement that I might have wondered if I'd imagined it, but Floss made it clear that I hadn't.

"I wasn't planning on going home," she said in clear, clean syllables. I know I wasn't the only one who saw El Jeffery wince, and in my limited experience, it's not that easy to tell when a griffin winces.

"You do have that option," El Jeffery said. "But Fred was talking about you just yesterday." Floss didn't say a word. El Jeffery added, "He'll know you're here, just like I did. He'll feel it. And he did say how much he missed you."

Floss jiggled her shoulders and shook her head, while Lucia said, "Freddy?" on a little sigh.

Floss focused on Lucia. "He'll certainly know I'm here if I'm with Lucia," she said in a thoughtful, measured way, and Lucia blushed.

"He does worry. And he's nothing like the rest," El Jeffery said in a low voice. He seemed to be addressing only the question of Fred and ignoring completely the idea of Lucia and Fred. That was too bad, because Lucia with some unknown named Fred suddenly seemed like a topic of high interest to me.

Then, as if he were saying something delicate in mixed company, possibly something in poor taste as well, he added, "Feron may feel it too, you know."

"Mmph," Floss said, which for Floss was almost no statement at all.

"Feron?" Nicholas asked.

Floss glared at him and he tilted his head to the side, eyes wide. "I'm just curious because you sort of growled."

"Older brother," El Jeffery said. "Didn't she mention him?"

"She didn't mention family much at all," Nicholas said.

"Maybe because it's no one else's business?" Floss asked on a long sigh.

Nicholas held up a hand. "That's probably true." Then he grinned. "But it'd be hard to not be interested. Still, pax."

"Double pax," El Jeffery added, both paws up.

Floss shook her head, and when she answered El Jeffery she skipped over Feron and right over Fred and Lucia, too. "Before we worry about bicycles and my family, let's get food. I plan much better on a full stomach, and even though I'm always famished before a show, I can never eat."

"Famished before, famished after," Tonio bantered.

"Famished during a show," El Jeffery added.

Tonio turned toward him, hand in the air, and they high-fived. Tonio's hand looked like a miniature marshmallow against El Jeffery's pie-sized paw.

Floss tried to look mad and ended up giggling. I think it was the first time I'd ever heard Floss giggle.

Nicholas was the only one who held back as we started a walking train that followed Floss and El Jeffery. When I realized he wasn't with me I glanced back and raised my eyebrows. "Are you coming?"

He dragged his feet as he came up to me. "Faerie seems very cool. But I just thought—Faerie food?" he whispered. "You know, eat it and stay here forever? Sort of like a superpsychedelic experience that never ends?"

Floss heard, even though I almost didn't. Fey must have ears like street kids. Always wide open. She turned back and said, "Don't worry. That only happens if we let it. You're with us."

El Jeffery chimed in, "You'll be perfectly safe." And hungry as I was, I decided there was no reason not to believe them.

"Because, really," I said to Nicholas, continuing my thought out loud, "it's just Floss, after all."

XIII

"Mélange. Just like the world."

$\mathscr{F}$aerie food was safe. Faerie food was delicious. And it seemed to be in endless supply at Dau Hermanos, the Welsh-Mexican-themed diner where Floss and El Jeffery took us that afternoon.

Dau Hermanos seemed to be a sort of old-fashioned roadhouse. The front of the place nearly touched the cobbles that ran past it, and there was a huge, grassy, chalk-colored field with wildflowers in the back. The restaurant was on the ground floor, and there were rooms upstairs. Kind of a fey bed-and-breakfast.

"Because," Floss had said as we approached, "the two closest towns are that way"—she pointed past the hills to the north—"and that way." This time she pointed to the river running to the west. "This place is kind of centrally located."

I was curious. "What are the towns like?"

El Jeffery said, "Townish. Crowded. Harder to breathe and harder to see the sky. Especially at night."

"Romantic griffin," Floss said with a grin, and she opened the door.

The Dau Hermanos menu was six pages long. Buckets of fresh beer, ten different kinds of tacos, mountains of salad with lime-cilantro dressing, avocados, lamb empanadas, and gallons of tea. Mariachi music and bagpipes on the jukebox, wool capes on the walls, and red striped shawls on the tables.

Tonio's eyes shone happily, and I knew, because I knew Tonio, that he had to be drinking in the color and culture mash-up. Max, who had kept his menu after we'd ordered, was reading it over and over like it was a love letter. Lucia and Nicholas looked relaxed, and El Jeffery and Floss looked as happy as I felt with the food spread out in front of us.

I waved my hand through the air, trying to encompass the Dau Hermanos experience. "So," I said to

Floss and El Jeffery, "does this kind of mix and match happen here a lot?"

Floss chewed a stray tortilla chip drenched in fish salsa and nodded. "We cross the border a lot. At least"—she glanced at El Jeffery—"some of us do."

"It's not my fault," he said, calm and slow. "I tend to stand out more when I'm not in Faerie."

"If you'd practice glamouring," Floss said, and stopped as if she'd actually completed the sentence.

"It's just so much work. You know how lazy I am." He shrugged, but there was a definite grin settled on his beak.

"Foolish griffin," Floss said. She smiled as she slapped him on the foreleg. "You're not lazy at all. You just don't really want to go."

"There is that," he agreed.

"But other people?" I persisted. "They go?"

"Most come back," El Jeffery said, with a glance at Floss. "Most just want a quick look, a taste. They take what they like, then bring it back here. And you get this." He pointed to the Dau Hermanos menu still clutched in Max's hands.

"You make it sound easy. Does it work like that going the other way? Because Floss, you had to bring us through. We couldn't do it on our own. You said it was hard to do that. Like when Nicholas wanted to come and couldn't make it work."

"It's not easy," Floss said, stretching out the words, "but we all know it's not impossible." She glanced at Lucia, then added, "Mostly, if you're alone, you require that strong need that we talked about before. Or a strong emotion. You sort of wish yourself through."

A look I couldn't read flashed across Lucia's face. "If you're lucky, you end up in the right place," she said in a soft voice.

I thought about what Floss had said. "So Major could do that? We're not safe here, after all?" Everyone looked at me, and I added, "He's got strong emotion, that's for sure."

But Floss shook her head and looked frustrated. "It's not like that. Even if he tried to use hate or anger to wish himself through, it's still tricky. And hate and anger are always skinny, weak emotions. They're not easy to work with. Really, chances of him getting through with those are almost nil."

"Unless he's connected with a sponsor," El Jeffery added.

Floss stopped eating. She looked thoughtful. "There's certainly been fey activity back home. Remember that last influx of dust and drinks? That had a fey edge to it. And there was that presence I thought I felt."

"I remember that," I said. "We talked about it. But you said you couldn't pin it down. You said it wasn't anything to worry about."

"I know, I know." She looked thoughtful, but then she shook her head. "No." She seemed positive. "No, I don't see how that has any connection with Major."

"Maybe Major's a dust dealer," I said, excited.

But now Tonio shook his head. He blew out a soft, one-syllable laugh. "There's no way. Something like that would involve a lot of work. Networks, employees, travel. And money. You'd have to have a good-sized bankroll to start that kind of an operation. As much as he wants power, Major doesn't work if he doesn't have to, and he'd never spend a cent on something that wasn't a sure thing. And even if it was a sure thing, the payoff would have to be extraordinary or he wouldn't take the risks. Major's only goal is to benefit Major, and I can't see anyone giving him enough of an incentive to risk a run-in with the law."

I still liked my theory. "You said he'd been traveling," I told Floss.

She snorted. "Your guesses of Alabama and Greece were better than a guess for Faerie."

"He's been really busy annoying us," Max said. "Where would he find the time to gather drinks and dust, let alone get a distribution network going?"

"And to get through on his own, using hate as a passport?" El Jeffery said, making it sound like a question. "The damage factor would be quite high, I think." He tapped a talon on the table to emphasize his point.

Nicholas wrapped my hand in his. He bumped my leg with his own, a sweet version of footsie. Both things blew Major right out of my mind. I slid my chair so close to Nicholas that I could feel his body heat, and I held tight to his hand. He grinned at me. "Relax, Persia. We're fine. Can't you feel it?"

Tonio nodded and said, "Listen to Nicholas. He's a smart guy."

Max grinned and even winked.

All the messages coming my way were clear and clean. Everyone seemed calm and blissful. It appeared to be working for them, so I decided "Why not?" and I squeezed Nicholas's fingers in my own as an affirmation.

A tall, slender, ethereal man came to our table, followed by a squat, barrel-chested gentleman.

"Floss!" said the tall one. "You're home. I knew it! I would have been here earlier, but the kitchen wanted me."

"If that's where you were, it was time well spent. The food was fabulous." She pointed at all of us. "I brought my friends," she said. Then she nodded at the two men. "These are the brothers this place is named for. Bron"—she pointed at the tall one—"and Rohan."

Names were exchanged like packages on a holiday

morning, and then Nicholas asked the obvious question. "Brothers?"

Rohan laughed. "In name."

"Which is generally so much stronger than blood," said Bron.

Tonio said, "Mélange. Just like the world."

I looked at my friends, old and new, and felt relaxed and calm. As soon as I realized that, I also realized that I was so tired that I didn't think my eyes would stay open a moment longer. From a distance I heard Floss say, "I think we're going to need a few rooms. . . ."

I woke feeling like I'd slept for a year or two, and I let the thoughts of Faerie food slip through my mind one more time. This time I wasn't worried. This time I just wondered if it was a very fine restorative, and then I decided not to wonder so much, to just let the good feelings flow along.

The window in my room was opened an inch or two. There was a breeze blowing through that smelled of clover and dandelions. And cocoa mulch, too, that reminded me of the chocolate factory we'd left behind. The breeze slipped past Lucia, where she slept in the bed next to mine, and ruffled her hair like a lover.

I stretched three good, long yoga stretches, and shoved back the covers. It wasn't until I was fully out of bed, glancing down at a T-shirt I couldn't recall putting on the night before, that I remembered the only thing I had to wear was the dinner dress from the last scene of *B&B*. Then next to the door I saw a chair piled high with clothes. I dug through the jumble and found jeans and a shirt with the Dau Hermanos logo—a triskelion topped by a flat-brimmed Mexican hat. I dressed and left the room, pulling the door closed so softly that I didn't even hear the lock snick.

There were no clocks in the dining room of Dau Hermanos, but the way the light filtered through the windows made me think it was very late morning. There were no calendars, either, but I was pretty sure it was tomorrow, as long as I believed I'd left home yesterday. Then I saw the ethereal guy from the night before. He was called something very fey, so not John or Ron, but—Bron. That was it, or at least I thought that was it.

Still, I wasn't so positive that I was going to risk using the name. When I said, "Hi," I just let the name slide. No point in irritating my host. Then, even though I probably sounded like an addled human, I tacked on, "You wouldn't happen to know what day it is, would you?"

He looked amused. "Wednesday."

Mindful that I was standing in a Faerie diner, I said cautiously, "The day after yesterday?" and he laughed. Someone that fragile-looking shouldn't have a laugh involving snorts. He brought it under control faster than I would have been able to, but there was still a lingering smile when he said, "That's an ambivalent question, isn't it?"

Maybe it was the laugh. Maybe it was the casual way he leaned against the breakfast bar. More probably it was the way he hooked one long, elegant foot around the leg of a stool and placed it, with perfect precision, right in front of me. He just put me at ease. I climbed up on the stool and said, "Ambivalent. Okay.

But I'm still not too clear on where and when I am."

"Faerie food."

I jumped up, all that nice relaxation gone—snap—and looked for an escape route.

"No, no." He waved his long-fingered hands at me. They moved like he was sketching pictures in the air, and he looked frustrated. "That's not what I meant. Look, let's start over."

"Hmm." I wasn't ready to commit, but I sat down, on the very edge of the stool.

He bowed to me, as if I were royalty. "Persia. Welcome to Dau Hermanos, the best Welsh-Mex restaurant in Faerie."

"Just how many of those are there, then?" I muttered.

His grin was wicked when he said, "One." And he laughed again.

"Now," he continued, "about fey food. I only meant that it can make you sleep the sleep of the just and righteous. You wake feeling rejuvenated."

I had to agree with that. But, "I won't have to stay here forever? Until I die and my bleached bones are buried in the far, far hills?"

He raised both eyebrows. "What *have* you been reading?"

I blushed. He smiled and said, "Or should I just say only if you want to?"

Still able to feel the flush on my face I said, "Yeah, that might be better."

"Consider it said."

"Right. Okay."

"And now, what will you eat? The breakfast crowd leaves by nine and we reopen at one, but I can certainly find something if you tell me what you'd like."

"Eggs?" I guessed.

"Certainly. And . . . ?"

Twenty minutes later I had a platter of food that I wasn't sure I'd even make a dent in, and eighteen minutes after that it was gone. During those eighteen minutes I'd confirmed that yes, he really was Bron, he'd known Floss for years (a look here that made me wonder just what "known" meant), and he held strong feelings of dislike for her privileged family, all except for Fred, his best friend. He also said that he'd gone to cooking school in Vermont. "The winters were as cold and snowy as here, and the summers were just as hot, but I couldn't stay. I loved it, but I missed here too much. I came back home."

"Not like Floss," I said.

"Oh, she misses it. She just can't stomach the family pride line, their we-have-the-power-and-we'll-do-as-we-please way of ruling."

I chewed thoughtfully on my last bite of tortilla. "They rule the whole world?"

Bron coughed in surprise. He opened and closed his mouth twice. Words seemed to want to come out, but they didn't quite make it. He finally said, "Mab, no. Just this bit. Persia, have you no idea of the breadth of Faerie?"

"Actually, no, I really don't. Floss and Lucia never explained."

Bron blew out a breath. "Probably because it's rather complicated. If someone gets a degree in Faerie history, it takes twice as long as a degree in anything else."

"Not a popular program, then?"

"On the contrary. There are waiting lists to get in. The extremely short version is that there are pieces of Faerie scattered all over the world. Some are connected, some bounce off each other, and some are so far removed from all others that they're often unreachable. Generally, fey can travel back and forth. Humans, even those brought here as friends, not much at all.

"These pieces often tap your world. When they do, it's easier to find a way to move between."

"The bubble theory." I was excited. This part I kind of understood.

When Bron said, "Bubble theory?" I gave him the "magic passes through" school of thought.

He tipped his head to one side, considered, and then said, "Close enough."

"So, Floss's parents rule this bubble," I said, "and it bumps against my world?"

"For now, at least."

I looked at Bron. "That was oblique."

"They shift sometimes."

I straightened and swallowed. "We won't be able to get home?"

"It hasn't happened for a long time." He sounded encouraging.

"Oh, great. Like 'the volcano hasn't erupted for a long time.'" I stood up. "I'm a little nervous now, just in case you want to know that."

"Floss has a very strong connection with your place in the world."

"Um."

He nodded and patted my hand.

I wasn't all that reassured by the pat, but I couldn't think of anything to do to feel more confident of my chances of getting home. Then I thought that since I was already nervous, I might as well get all the rest of the scary stuff out of the way too. "And the corner-of-the-eye creatures? How do they play in?"

Bron blinked, then said, "Just how safe is your world, Persia?"

He had me there. "Point," I said, because it surely was. "So I just shouldn't worry?"

He laughed. "No. You should always worry, at least enough to be safe. It's just like where you came from. Blood and flowers. Dragons and windigos."

"That's not quite how I would have described things."

"Every place has its challenges."

It was my turn to laugh. "I guess so. Me, I'm just a bookbinder and an actor who sometimes helps put puppets together."

His ears perked up. Literally. I saw the points rise. "Bookbinder?"

I explained about the Outlaw programs and my periodic forays into box-making, embossing, and other paper arts.

"Mmm." He looked excited, the way he might look after tasting a particularly good flan. Then he said, "Menus."

"Menus?"

"Something substantial, with a way to keep updating specials and drinks and such. I find some very amazing drinks on your side of the world." When I didn't say anything he added, "I'd pay you, of course. And I swear it wouldn't be in Faerie gold."

"Are you offering me a job?"

"Well, yes. Didn't I just say?"

I grinned. "Sort of, I guess. And yes, I'd love to

try my hand at that."

"At what?" Floss rattled down the steps, followed by Nicholas and Tonio. They all looked so easy, so carefree, that I almost had to look twice to make sure they were my friends.

"Persia, that's great," Nicholas said after I'd explained. But his eyes were more on my empty plate than they were on me. Bron noticed. "Anyone else hungry?" he asked, and after that there was a flurry of activity as more Outlaws and one griffin (everyone was here by now) made an ever-changing amoeba of people and food.

The plates had almost been licked clean when Rohan came in, apron slung over his shoulder. He stopped in the doorway, took in the mess in the dining room, and sighed, huge and heavy. It was the sound I imagined a weary dragon would make. He said, "Lunch crowd due soon," and sighed again.

Bron patted Rohan's shoulder and looked sympathetic. "I'll take care of it. Don't worry."

Rohan widened his eyes. "All by yourself?"

Bron laughed. "Well . . ."

So close on Bron's words that he almost crushed them under his boots came a male version of Floss.

"Freddy," Lucia said on an exhale that sounded like a soft spring breeze shuffling through new daffodils.

Floss's eyes snapped up, and then her body followed her eyes. She made it across the floor of the inn in three huge steps and flung her arms around that male version of herself. Even if Lucia hadn't said his name, I would have guessed that this was Fred. He even had Floss's dandelion fluff hair.

"Missed me, then?" he asked.

"I always do."

"You could stay home." Fred sounded a little wistful, but Floss must not have heard that. She pulled back like she'd been licked by a fireplace flame, stiff and ramrod straight.

"I didn't come back to tread old ground."

Fred held up both hands, palms out. "Peace, peace. I'm not asking you to. It was only an observation."

"And a really low-key one, Floss." Lucia was standing next to the two of them, throwing dagger glances at Floss while Nicholas and I watched, eyes wide open, so we wouldn't miss a thing.

"Hello, Lucia," Fred said. There was a tone in his voice that hadn't been there when he'd talked to Floss, a gentleness, almost a caress. Apparently Lucia wasn't the only one who was interested.

But now Tonio and Max were on their feet, shaking hands with Fred. Nicholas and I made sure we were part of the introductions too, and soon the room took on the atmosphere of a closing-night party—which it sort of was, because we'd certainly closed ourselves down the night before.

Bits and pieces of sentences kept drifting my way. I let them wash over me, almost like words from a poem. Bicycles, bridges, troll, titanium, feathers, kites, gloss, clown white, manor, fighting, explosions, sheep. If I could put it all together, I could write a haiku, or some little stream-of-conciousness couplets.

I sat, the words swirled, and I was content, so content that it almost felt illegal, just like a pink drink. I was fed. I was warm and dry. I had my friends. It all seemed like just enough. I thought, So this is Faerie. Why didn't we come a long time ago?

XIV

"Reginald," he said.

The troll came just before the lunch rush. By sheer will and, I was sure, pieces of magic, Bron and Rohan had cleaned the place after our breakfast only to have it start to fill up almost immediately with a new group of hungry, thirsty people. I'd been staying in the background, studying the early lunch crowd. I thought they were amazing. For the first time in my life I was seeing people with six-fingered hands, people with iridescent wings tucked beneath bright orange backpacks, people that stood as tall as my knee and no taller. I watched surreptitiously as they filtered in, and I saw something else, too. They all seemed like decent people, people trying to get through life. Just like us. Just like most of the people back home.

Then in came the troll.

He was short and broad, and he smelled vaguely of river water and dried blood. When he said, "Lucia," he sounded like a cave would sound if it could talk.

Nicholas said, low-voiced, "Um, remember those eye-corner creatures? Do you think that's one? Because even though I can see him straight on, he's scary as hell."

"I don't know," I said, my voice as quiet as his, "but you're right about scary. Maybe even terrifying." I looked for someone to ask, but there was no one, because they were all too busy with their own troll reactions.

Lucia had frozen. Completely. Her eyes didn't even blink. I saw Floss jump to her feet, saw El Jeffery lumber up, his beak snapping. I saw Rohan start to move across the room in a fast walk, still carrying a tray of deep brown beers. I saw early lunchers look around, nervous and unsure. What I didn't see was how Fred got to the door before anyone else.

"Reginald," he said. The word sounded bitter and barely civil.

The troll stepped to one side. Fred might as well have been invisible for all the attention Reginald paid to him.

Fred stepped back into the troll's path. "Reginald," he repeated. "What brings you here?"

"Flautas? Haggis?" asked Bron. He must have moved like Fred. Not there one second, there the next. The two of them stood shoulder to shoulder. Together like that, they looked massive. I was glad I wasn't on the receiving end of the glares on their respective faces.

Two must have been too much to ignore. Reginald stopped, and Fred nodded. "Thank you. May I repeat, what are you doing here?"

All of us seemed to be carefully pretending that we hadn't heard Lucia's name being mentioned in that cavernous voice. Even Reginald. He just said, in flat words that made the room shake, "It's lunchtime. I'm hungry."

"Tacos? Shepherd's pie?" suggested Bron.

"To go," added Fred.

"You can't make me." Reginald's words sounded like they belonged to a whiny six-year-old. A big, probably dangerous, whiny six-year-old.

"I'm not making you do anything," Fred said. "I'm only suggesting. To go?" But the question had a hard, clean edge.

Reginald had to have felt it, because I could feel it. The room wasn't on his side. If he moved the wrong way, I had the feeling a lot of other people were going to move too, and they'd all converge on the same spot—the spot where Reginald was standing.

Apparently even trolls have their moments of brightness. Reginald let his wide, dark eyes scan the room. They were deep, those eyes, with long lashes, and unaccountably pretty. I remembered Floss's comment about trolls and bad eyesight, but Reginald's eyes were good enough to let him find Lucia. He settled his sight on her for a long time and finally said, "Fish tacos. Crisps. Two tankards of Summer's Rest Weiss." Then he shifted his gaze right onto Fred and added, "To go."

Fred smiled. Bron walked to the kitchen, toe-heel, facing forward, while moving backward. Reginald simply stood and took up a large amount of floor space.

Bron was back so fast it almost felt like he hadn't been gone. The to-go bag he held was decorated with the Dau Hermanos logo—the same one that was on my shirt. The bag was huge. I thought it was because of the tankards of beer. But when Bron said, "I put in a few extras. I know how hungry trolls can get," and Rohan came up behind him with a second bag colored silver and with a different logo that said "Keep It Cold," I knew the first bag was all food.

"Whoa," I mumbled.

"Yeah," Nicholas agreed. He was so close to me that his breath tickled my ear.

Reginald must have heard, and he must have understood just what we were implying. He swung his head around and looked straight at us. I understood then why Lucia had frozen. Those beautiful eyes were also cold and hard and blank. Nicholas stepped in front of me, maybe to block the look in those eyes, maybe to keep Reginald from really seeing me. Whatever it was for, I was glad it had happened. I leaned in to Nicholas's back for support and felt him steady himself against me. Double moral support.

At any other time I would have enjoyed that feeling, his body next to mine. Right then all I felt was a huge sense of relief that I wasn't standing there with those eyes of Reginald's focused on me.

The troll dropped money on a nearby table. He didn't ask the price and neither Bron nor Rohan named it. Then he took his food and walked out. The floor shook beneath his cement-heavy footsteps.

Once he was gone, the room itself seemed to exhale and to expand. Conversations started up again. I saw someone with ear points wave her hands in what looked like a Reginald shape, and shake her head. Her companions, one gnarled as a tree trunk and one with the same see-through presence as Floss, nodded. I heard all three of them sigh just the way kids in a lunchroom sigh when the class problem walks in and out of their view.

Tonio and Floss both turned to Lucia, but it was

Fred who got to her first, crossing the room again in that way I couldn't see. His arm was around her shoulders, and she clung to him like a lifeline. Floss moved to intercept them as Fred started Lucia on a slow walk toward the kitchen, but Fred shook his head, and Bron dropped one hand on Floss's arm. Floss stopped, and Bron tugged her toward an empty table.

"Aren't trolls supposed to turn people into stone?" Nicholas's breath moved my hair and tickled my ear.

I looked up, to my left. "I think it's that they turn into stone themselves. That one certainly could."

"No, he couldn't. For all the emotion I'd ever seen from him before Lucia, I'd have thought he might be able to," said Rohan. "But he can't. I know for a fact. He used to practice, you know. When he was a trolling. He could never get it."

"What would be the point of that exercise, anyway?" Nicholas asked.

Rohan shrugged. "Fear factor. And strength. It's very hard to hurt stone."

"I would think he'd be hard to hurt just the way he is," I said.

Rohan glanced toward the kitchen. "Not really. Lucia managed it without ever trying."

"Different kind of hurt," I said.

"But just as lethal," said Rohan. "Reginald is very enamored of your friend."

"I don't think she's too thrilled about that," I said, in what I considered a dramatic understatement.

"Trolls often take what they can't get," said Rohan.

I looked at him. "You don't have a brother or a cousin or something who runs a stationery store, do you? He's the only other person I know who speaks in one-offs."

Rohan grinned again, wide and wicked. "Fey blood runs everywhere," he said grandly.

Nicholas shook his head. "You're saying we should watch out for Lucia."

"We should all watch out for one another," he said, and followed Fred's path to the kitchen.

Floss and Bron must have discussed the Reginald situation in more depth than Nicholas, Rohan, and I had. They actually had a plan.

"Fabulous," said Tonio. "Let's hear it. Reginald seems to have all too much in common with Major. What works with one might work with the other. I'm all ears."

We were sitting around a very large, disc-shaped table the color of old putty. It took up a good portion of floor in the middle of the Dau Hermanos dining room.

"Like the Knights of the Round Table," Nicholas said, looking pleased.

"I," said El Jeffery, "shall be King Arthur."

Floss sighed. I could feel it in my feet, it was so deep. "Could we move on?"

"Spoilsport," the griffin murmured.

She just grinned. "When you decide to play someone other than the king I won't say a word."

"Snap," he said, and she patted his paw.

"Tonio's right about Reginald and Major," Floss said, "but Reginald's dangerous in a different way. Major's subtle. He has finesse."

"Reginald's a boor, a bully. The kind who works on sheer strength and no brain," Max said, sounding sure of himself. "I've met a lot of people like him. They're actually much harder to deal with than people who think. It's almost like they're looking for pain."

I saw Lucia shiver. I saw Fred's arm slide around her. I thought that stupid old adage, "out of the fire" blah, blah, blah, wasn't so stupid, after all. And I asked, "Are we in more trouble than we were before?"

"Not more. Different," Max said.

"Right. Exactly," said Bron. "The thing on our side is that Reginald is a known entity. He's big. He's easy to spot. And he's just not that bright. We keep Lucia close to one of us at all times, preferably with someone who's more fey than not."

Fred snuggled Lucia close to him. "I volunteer."

"My, what a surprise," Bron said, but he smiled when he said it. "You Outlaws," he continued, "just keep doing whatever it is you do, or planned to do while you were here. You don't need to be trapped in nothingness because of one troll."

"And if things progress any further," said Fred, "Bron and I will have a small chat with him. I'm sure he'll listen, aren't you?" The glance he cast at Bron glittered like a finely honed blade.

I actually pulled back a bit, but by the time my shoulders had shifted, Fred's look was gone. I'd just managed to convince myself that it didn't mean what I thought it meant when Max reached toward Bron and said, "I could help talk to him." Bron and Fred clasped hands with Max, their arms like wheel spikes around that big disc table, and I knew my first impression had been the right one. The three of them were like crossed swords, ready for battle.

I almost felt sorry for Reginald.

XV

**"It may simply have been because
of bicycle theater."**

*A*fter his one appearance Reginald wasn't
seen again, and I let him drift off to a holding cell, one of those places in your mind that you
know is there but that you don't access much. The
thought of him nudged me every once in a while, but
it was never enough of a nudge to do anything about.
Everyone else seemed to be acting the same way. Out
of sight, out of mind, more or less. Or, it may simply
have been because of bicycle theater.

So far that consisted of late-night discussions,
technical meetings, laments about lighting, and
loud moans about costumes. It was taking up an

unaccountable amount of our time, but not in a bad way. More as if this was what we'd come to Faerie for all along, and we wanted to mount the best possible show for this new breed of audience.

Nicholas worried about the portability of lights. Max and Lucia muttered about the computer they'd left behind, and went back to old-style tickets and accounting methods. Floss swore softly about ankle skirts catching in bicycle chains, which I didn't understand. Why ankle skirts when we didn't even know who was what? But that was just Floss. Tonio paced and thought, and paced and thought. He'd discarded the "let's play ourselves" plan on the grounds that it was too predictable and was now trying to come up with something truly memorable.

"*Midsummer Night's Dream* from the fey perspective," he tried.

Floss sent one hard look his way and said, "It already is. And no."

Tonio paced more.

I was already at work, but my work was for Bron and Rohan. I'd scoured our little corner of Faerie, looking for book boards and cloths. I'd practiced and discarded most of the bindings I knew how to make and was searching for a way to meet Bron's main requirement: easy to update. No plastic sleeve was my own requirement. Plastic is not good for birds, beasts, or menus.

Bron himself came and hovered over my shoulder so often that I finally said, "I feel like I have a way-ward guardian angel," which made Rohan laugh and say, "Guardian something, perhaps, but I think you missed the mark with angel."

Bron only said, "Feel however you like. Just make me menus."

I flipped my latest attempt onto its stomach and rapped its back with my knuckles. It flopped down on the table, flat, like an obedient dog playing dead. I looked at it in surprise, then said, "Well. That seems to work."

Bron reached a long arm over my head. He turned the book over, then closed, opened, and closed it with a snap. "And how do you update, change the specials? I refuse to add those little extra sheets that get lost and dropped and trampled underfoot."

"No. Look." I was excited. "You pull these." I slipped the thick silver—real silver—pins from the spine. "And voilà! Add what you need, take out what you don't, and push in the pins. . . ." I held it up, all together again, and beamed at Bron.

He fiddled with my book for a few more seconds. "Persia, this is so much better than what we have. It's genius. And so are you."

I grinned. "Did everyone hear that? Genius."

Floss snorted, but she smiled at the same time.

El Jeffery, who'd been busy modeling those ankle skirts for Floss said, "Impressive."

Tonio said, "Of course you are, darling. We all knew," and paced back to the other side of the room.

Max, who was obviously involved in other things, said, "What about a slide rule?" and Lucia said, "Max, I don't know a thing about slide rules. But if you do, it'll at least work here. We'd never have to worry about electricity."

A much better reaction came from Nicholas, and it was also the sweetest. He leaned over, kissed me on the nose, then moved down and bussed me on the cheek. "Brilliant" was all he said, but I felt like I was ten years old and had been given a pony.

We may not have had a play, but we did have bicycles, two slick silver purple things that gleamed like summer rain. And we had one flat, gray, ratty unicycle that didn't gleam at all and looked as if it never had.

El Jeffery, of all people, showed up on the unicycle the afternoon after my triumph with the menus. He was followed by Fred, riding one bicycle and leading the other. Or maybe "leading" wasn't quite the right word. It was more that the second bicycle trailed him like a puppy learning to heel.

The first words out of Floss's mouth were, "Do they know you took them?"

Fred apparently didn't need to ask who "they" were. "They don't even have any idea you're here as far as I can tell. They're not tuned into you like El Jeffery and I are."

Floss snorted. "They're not tuned into me at all."

Fred shrugged and seemed to know there wasn't

anything else to say. He and his two bicycles had stopped directly in front of Dau Hermanos. The riderless one stood at attention behind Fred's rear wheel. Magic. I watched it enviously. I couldn't stand that straight on two feet, and I was beginning to feel tested in the worst way by the magical things all around me. Balancing bicycles, for example. It was like the air in Faerie was extra-ionized, making anything possible. It made me feel as if I should be doing something strange and wonderful. I wondered briefly just what that thing might be, then let it go. The something would either show itself or it wouldn't. I didn't think I could force it.

Then Floss asked, "What about Feron?"

"Our beloved brother? You expect him to be paying attention to you?" Fred laughed with no humor. "You've been gone longer than I thought, then. Think about it. Fer is, and always has been, only concerned with Fer. You don't need to worry about him."

"On the contrary. I haven't been gone that long, and I don't expect him to know about me. I just don't know if he has spies. And I always worry about him.

It's smart to worry about the people you don't trust. It keeps them in the front of your mind so that you recognize it right away if they try something sneaky."

Fred shook his head. "No spies as far as I know. And he's hardly been around for months. I don't know where he has been, but it's not here. Leave him out of the equation."

Floss didn't look convinced, but all she did was say "Hmm."

The exchange made me wonder again about their family, the one that ruled things. Since this was something I'd mulled over on and off ever since Floss had said that ruling was their job, I decided to go ahead and try to find out more. I said, very carefully, "Floss, your family might be happy to see you."

Even as the words came out of my mouth I wasn't sure I was saying something true. I thought of my own family and what my answer would be if someone said this to me. Still, there was something so intriguing about the mystery of Fred and Floss and those parents. And now there was the brother to add to the mix.

Fred winced at my statement, and his follow-me bike crashed to the ground. El Jeffery swung off his unicycle with more grace than any griffin should have been able to master and built a protection around Floss that was almost visible. Lucia said, "Think, Persia. You're in the same position," which made me wish I'd kept my mouth shut more than anything else had.

But Nicholas said, "It's a fair question, actually."

Fred sighed, but he agreed. "It actually is, you know."

Floss growled. Floss glowered. Then Tonio slid an arm around her shoulders. "If you tell them, they all will quit asking. And it might exorcise the demons. Look at me and Major."

"I don't have another hidey-hole," Floss muttered. "I lost that."

That seemed like a sideways statement until I noticed that Tonio was looking straight at Floss. Just looking and breathing deep, calming breaths. He breathed and he waited until Floss blushed and stared at her toes. Then he said, "We all lost it. And it wasn't our fault. But we also all knew where we stood and we dealt with it together."

"Maybe I don't want to deal with it together."

"Does it affect our work here? Our existence?" That was Max.

Floss turned her eyes on him and stayed that way for a long time. The rest of us seemed to hold our collective breaths. When she said, "It might. Possibly," the words seemed to be dragged out of her throat.

"Maybe we all need to sit down and chat," Fred said in a soft voice, and Floss sighed one more long breath and nodded.

WHAT'S GOING ON IN FLOSS AND FRED'S FAMILY

Rulers aren't always fair or just. Example: The last town that didn't follow royal directives and instead ran their own candidate in the regional election was moved to another corner of Faerie. Far, far away.

Floss has taken exception, since she was tiny, to the we're-better-than-you style of ruling practiced by her family. Example: At Floss's fourth birthday party she was given a gift that wasn't on the "suggested" list written by her mother. The child who gave the gift was told to never associate with Floss again. "She was one of my best friends," Floss said. She seemed far away when she added, "And I did so love that stuffed werecreature."

Both Fred and Floss believe that their mother is responsible for much of the bad style of rule that affects their world because . . .

Both know that their father is more involved in grand issues than small ones. "He doesn't pay attention," Floss said, and her frustration was evident. Example: A 0.01 percent increase in taxes seems like such a small thing that it almost gets lost in the record-keeping shuffle. Do it every year, though, and the money becomes significant. Because it's easy to hide, it's also easy to keep. Floss's mother has always kept it. Floss's father has never seemed to notice.

Almost everyone Floss cares about is well out of the ruling class and their struggles—unnecessary ones, she believes—drive her crazy. Example: El Jeffery's family has been living on the edge forever. Griffin families are large. There's never enough money or anything else, and those taxes keep rising.

So she left. Fred, who feels much like Floss, stayed and tried to fix things at home. Neither approach has made much of a difference.

Brother and sister still see change as inevitable, but inevitable seems to be getting further away all the time. Example: Their father is gone more and more, for longer periods of time, serving the Group Council in ever-increasing positions of responsibility. His wife encourages him to run for those responsible positions in each election, and she also makes sure that he gets the votes he needs to win.

Fred is continually treading a line of subversion that seems very thin. Example: Last year he quietly campaigned for his father's opponent. It made no difference in the election outcome, but Fred felt like he was being watched all the time. He still occasionally feels like he's treading on very swampy ground.

Floss will not be welcomed home with open arms. Example: Three years ago she tried to talk to her

mother about her concerns and was nearly ban-
ished from Faerie.

No one knows where Feron stands on any issue that
doesn't involve him, but on all issues that do involve
him, it's Feron first, last, and always. Example:
Feron was the first person to suggest permanent
banishment for Floss as punishment for speaking
out against the family rule. Later, El Jeffery over-
heard Feron saying that if Floss were gone, there
would be that much more for him to inherit.

"So," Floss finished in a swirl of understatement, "it becomes complicated."

I nodded because she was completely right.

Tonio said, "Not so much like Major after all."

"Much more internal," Max agreed. "Bigger and smaller at the same time."

What more could we say? Quiet covered us like a soft, wooly blanket. Until El Jeffery, like a savior, said, "Do you need music for this production? Because, fetching as I am in ankle skirts of variegated hues, I think my talents would be better employed in providing the musical theme."

Floss grinned. "And what would that be?"

"What would the production be?" he asked. "If someone can answer that I think we might start to coalesce."

Tonio coughed just enough to make us all look in his direction. "I keep turning the old fairy tales around and around. They've worked for us before, and here it should be a slam dunk. What if we did something with Mr. Fox? You know. The bold bridegroom, the doomed brides. It could become an allegory. Mr. Fox is the ruling class. The brides are commoners who keep losing to the ruler. Then the one bride who can beat him comes along and ends up victorious. And the ruling class tumbles."

"Ouch," said Fred.

"Hmm," said Floss.

"Maybe," said El Jeffery.

"How do we do it?" I asked.

"The silver road glowing in the moonlight," Nicholas said. "I could rig lights to make a road that sort of fades into the distance."

"Mr. Fox brings his newest bride to the house on a bicycle," sang Max.

"He lights the way with a lantern hanging from the handlebars," said Nicholas.

"Dead wife puppets," said Floss, getting into the spirit of the thing. "I can do that. Glow in the dark."

"The wife is in white," said Lucia. "She unicycles everywhere until she meets him, and then she's tamed to a bicycle."

"There are your ankle skirts, Floss," said El Jeffery, while Tonio repeated, " 'Tamed to a bicycle.' Nice phrase for a crackdown by the ruling class."

"And the house," I said. "The house can open and close like a giant book. A puppet-book house."

Fred shuffled his feet and looked uncomfortable. El Jeffery patted him on the arm with little pancake paw pats. But Floss said, "Let's try it. Let's see what happens." She looked at Fred. "It might be exactly what we've been looking for."

"It's a little more in-your-face than I was after," Fred said carefully.

"Sometimes it has to be," she said. "Anyway, they'll

probably never even know."

"If they won't know, why push it that hard?" Fred asked.

"Because even if they don't know, the commentary is there."

Tonio backed Floss. "You have to start somewhere," he said, which made me believe that he and Floss had talked about Faerie and rulers much more than I'd ever suspected.

Fred looked uncomfortable, then said, in the same careful way he'd spoken before, "Maybe you're right. Maybe so. But for now I think I'll just let you plan, and I'll go chat with Bron." As he faded away both of his bicycles snuggled together like puppies on the grass.

XVI

"Puppet karaoke!"

The upstairs rooms of Dau Hermanos began to resemble Max and Tonio's apartment. Floss had a room to herself. Most of the time the door was closed, but the bits of cloth and threads that bounced out whenever that door was opened, as well as the smell of glues, let everyone know that Floss was deep in the throes of creation.

Tonio was hunched over a small table in a room near the top of the stairs. The table was covered with coffee stains, ink smears, and pages of scribbles that I assumed would eventually become our script.

Max and Lucia sat together and mumbled what

sounded like magic words. Magic to me, at least, because I never could get a grasp on accounts payable. They also argued amiably about tickets and box office receipts until Lucia heard El Jeffery calling and went to practice unicycle riding.

In one corner of the largest upstairs room Nicholas worked with Fred. Fred and Bron had apparently hashed out Fred's reluctance to be "in-your-face," and Fred had become an honorary Outlaw. He and Nicholas were working on nonelectrical lighting effects, electricity being something that couldn't be counted on in Faerie.

"Maybe too modern?" Fred had suggested when Nicholas snarled over a previously-working-now-not-working-at-all outlet. "We have a long history that took place well before electricity was invented. Some things don't connect the way they should. Just like the electricity, actually." He sounded apologetic when he added, "I'm not sure why it comes and goes. It just does."

"Useless," Nicholas muttered. I was sure he wasn't talking about Fred because he was pointing at the offending outlet, the one with the new singe mark.

"We'll do it another way," Fred said. Yet another long, meandering discussion on alternate forms of lighting began.

Since Fred had been recruited less for his knowledge of lights and gels than for his knowledge of Faerie, his answers on electricity seemed not so good until I thought about it. I couldn't explain how electricity worked outside of Faerie. Why should he be able to explain how it didn't work inside?

Ideas about electricity aside, I was glad Fred was working with us. His presence made our choice of staging a play here, as well as our choice of material, feel honest and right.

I'd set myself up in the opposite corner of the room where I could work on various paper projects. It was nice to be near Nicholas, but I had another reason too. Listening to the exchanges between him and Fred, with the occasional visits from Bron, was like getting an abridged history lesson in fey life, past and present. And maybe future.

SOME OF THE THINGS I NOW KNOW
ABOUT FAERIE

Ruling factions fight for dominance just like at home.
Fey doesn't mean better than human.

Fey find humans as fascinating as humans find them.

Fey are very long-lived. Some are so long-lived they seem
to cross centuries, seem to make immortality a truth.

Magic and fey go together like toast and butter, like
science and humans. If it works in our world,
chances are good it won't work in Faerie.

Fred is sweet and Lucia should go out of her way to get
him. (Just a personal observation.)

If Fred and Floss have their way, this part of Faerie
will serve as a model, egalitarian society, but nei-
ther of them is sure what that model society will
look like.

Because history is history, the past will always affect
the future.

I was in my little corner working on menus when
I smelled burning and heard a pop that sounded like
a cork bouncing out of a bottle of something with

high levels of carbonation. I looked up and saw both Nicholas and Fred pressed against the wall, staring nervously at the small fire burning at their feet.

I jumped up, ready to stomp on the flames, when Fred waved his hand in the air, twisted his wrist, and breathed out a small puff of air. The fire died instantly. Fred breathed again, but this breath looked more like relief.

"I don't know, Nicholas," he said. He sounded regretful. "I told you I wasn't sure about that."

"It was just flash paper," Nicholas protested. "It shouldn't have done anything but flash. Poof."

"Remember where you are," Fred said.

"I do! I am! But we need to get some kind of lighting that flicks in and out. For the scene where the bride finds the vats of blood and bone. Like lightning."

"Let Floss make lightning," I said as I walked carefully across the floor.

"Floss is otherwise engaged," Fred said.

Nicholas nodded. "What he said. I need to figure this one out on my own."

I went to look for Floss. My arms were loaded with

menus for Bron, but I poked my head into Floss's new domain anyway. It looked much like the living room at Max and Tonio's place back home. I saw pieces of gold brocade, white lace, and cloth the color of the sky during an eclipse. I saw ankle boots and floating puppets in various stages of dismemberment. In one corner I saw a huge black box that looked like it wanted to transform into a house or a room but couldn't decide which was more effective.

Floss was on her back on the floor, eyes fixed on the ceiling where a wide-eyed, screaming face stared down at her. She was pointing at it and muttering, "No, I need you to be much more ethereal."

The face sighed.

I went downstairs and dropped the menus on the breakfast bar. Then I went back upstairs. I found Tonio bent over his desk making notes on a script that had obviously seen better days, which was interesting because he'd only been working on this thing for two days, tops. Nothing about this concept, from script to lights to puppets, seemed to be working.

"Hi," I said.

Tonio looked up, eyes narrow. Then he frowned at me and said, "Persia."

"Right," I said. I crouched next to him. "Listen, can I talk to you about this whole Mr. Fox thing?"

Those narrowed eyes opened wide, as if he were inviting questions.

"Floss is talking to disembodied heads; Nicholas is starting fires in an upstairs bedroom. The last I saw of her, Lucia was trying to learn how to ride a unicycle using El Jeffery for support. I'm making menus because I can't make posters or programs for a production with no name. Max is cutting out tickets with pinking shears. And you're holed up like a mad scientist inventing secret formulas." I waited a beat. "Where's the cohesion? Where's the all-for-one attitude? This doesn't feel very Outlaw to me, except maybe in the literal sense."

Tonio said, "You don't think this is going to work?"

"I didn't say that. I think there's a possibility that it's going to work just fine. It's just that right now it seems sort of . . ."

I searched for the best word while Tonio sighed

and collapsed in his chair. "Sloppy?" he supplied. "Slapdash? It seemed like a good idea when I came up with it."

"Yeah, it did. But now I'm not getting such a good feeling."

"Any suggestions?" He looked like he really wanted to know.

"Not me. All I can come up with is something blue. I keep seeing pale blue against night sky, but that could just be the program covers. Ask Floss."

Tonio shoved his papers aside and got up. "Why not?"

We went to visit Floss. With no preamble Tonio said to her, "Persia says this isn't working."

Floss rolled onto her side, propped herself up on one elbow, and said, "There's no fun in it. I think that's the problem."

"*The Bastard and the Beauty* wasn't all-out fun," I said.

Floss shrugged. "But it had moments of lightness. Quite a few, actually. This just seems bleak. And no," she added before we could speak, "it's not because it's my family we're prodding. They need prodding. It's just so . . ."

"Flat and dark?" I offered.

"The smart bride wins in the end," said Tonio, but he sounded like he was trying too hard.

"Right. But remember that review for *B&B* that we had? The one we all liked? 'Moralism without didacticism.' This whole thing seems to model school," I said. "It's like it's just trying too hard."

We sat on Floss's floor in a little circle. Dead wife puppets danced on their strings, moving on bursts of clove-and-arugula-scented air that blew through the windows.

Eventually Tonio tried, "Music and dance?"

Floss shook her head. "That doesn't mean less teachy."

"Other than sticking it to the royal family, what are we after?"

"Good question, Persia. Maybe that's where we should have started." Tonio stretched his neck and back, then shook his head. "I think I got so stuck looking for ideas that I lost the whole idea of the Outlaws."

"I don't think it has to be *très* Outlaw," I said. "It just has to be something we all like."

Nicholas walked in on the end of my sentence. Floss said, "Where's Fred?" and he shrugged. He looked tired. "I think he decided burning the place down wasn't such a good idea after all. He said he needed thinking room."

Tonio said, "I think we agree with him," just as Max and Lucia walked in together. Max was massaging his fingers, and Lucia had a bruise on her wrist and a bandage on her knee. They looked as tired as the rest of us.

"Oh, my," Tonio said after one careful look around the room. "This looks dire."

Max stretched out on the floor and sighed. "Is it Faerie that makes me so tired, or is it just that I'm not happy with what I'm doing right now?"

The question didn't seem to be directed to anyone in particular, but Floss answered. "Residual magic. It floats along and affects everyone it touches." Then she added, "But you may not like what you're doing, either."

Max closed his eyes and Tonio patted his head.

"If magic is the culprit, it does make some people

tired," Floss said, explaining further. "But there are others who get energized." She sounded like she was trying, and failing, to be peppy.

"Energized not working here," Nicholas muttered.

"It's not so obvious if you're fey." Now Floss sounded apologetic.

"We think Mr. Fox is a wash," Tonio said, in a sudden left turn.

Nicholas brightened up immediately. "Oh, good," he said, while Lucia dropped back on her elbows, winced, and breathed out a sigh that sounded like relief.

"Why didn't you all just tell me?" Tonio asked.

"I did," I said.

"Yes, you did. No one else bothered."

"I kept thinking it'd pull itself together," Floss said.

"Well, sure." Nicholas nodded at Floss. "You at least understand magic, which is probably the only thing we could have used to save it."

Lucia said, as if she were chatting to herself, "Karaoke."

Nicholas winced. "Oh, no. Karaoke is possibly the

saddest thing ever. You've obviously never been to a karaoke bar. People with absolutely no talent performing for an audience of drunks. It's painful. Not cute. Not funny. It just hurts."

I agreed. "Yeah, really, Lucia. I don't think so."

Lucia looked affronted. "Puppet karaoke," she said, as if that explained everything.

I heard a clicking in the hall that sounded like lion claws walking on wood, and then El Jeffery poked his head around the doorframe. "Lucia should not ride a unicycle," he said as his body followed his head. "No. Not at all. I, on the other hand, am quite accomplished on a unicycle. Did you know that I can even ride one while keeping a beat with a small drum? Perhaps a bodhran."

"Why do I have the feeling that you want to be in the play?" asked Floss.

"Even though said play exists in name only," added Tonio.

"It doesn't, you know," Max said, still in his prone position. When we all looked at him he shrugged. "We can't name it if we don't know what it is. And just for the record, I like the idea of puppet karaoke. Or I think I would if I knew how it worked. It sounds lighthearted. I could use some lighthearted."

"Yes!" Lucia held out her palm. Max reached one arm up from his stretched-out position on the floor and tapped her fingertips.

"Explain it, then," Tonio said, challenge in his voice. "Show us just how lighthearted it is."

Lucia made one hand into a bunny and began to sing "Mustang Sally." I giggled. I couldn't help it. The combination of the lyrics and a bouncy, double-eared finger rabbit just made me laugh. El Jeffery drummed a backbeat on the floor. Nicholas nodded along. Floss made her hand into an impromptu fish that danced with Lucia's rabbit. Max grinned up at Tonio. "How much more convinced do you need to be?"

"No more, really." Tonio laughed. It was great to hear that bassoon laugh. The mood in the room lifted right up. "Think of the puppets! We can do anything, because anything can sing karaoke." He glanced at me and Floss. "Remember my music and dance idea for Mr. Fox? That could translate nicely."

Lucia looked pleased with herself. She stopped singing and let her rabbit puppet turn back into a hand. Floss stopped being a fish while Max said, "What? Mr. Fox is a song-and-dance man?"

"No way," Floss said. "Not him. But she could be. The wife. She could be an actress. . . ."

"A music hall actress," I said. "We need a piano."

"We don't have a piano," Nicholas pointed out. "We appear to have a drum."

"That is correct," El Jeffery said. "But I can also do small cymbals. And bells."

"And my tambourine," Lucia said, sounding pleased.

"Oh!" Tonio snapped his fingers. "Mr. Fox could be the producer. That gives him power over her. And over the actresses before her."

"Money, money, money," sang Nicholas.

"Metaphorical death," said Max.

Floss called out, "Purple boas, lace gloves, and red berets."

This made even Tonio look a little nervous, but he just said, "That's an interesting interpretation."

"Blue. Something blue. Wigs. Skin. Anyway, I can get rid of all those body parts," Floss said. "It was getting creepy." She prodded Max on the foot. "Light-hearted. Just like you said. But with an edge."

"Twirl lights," Nicholas said. "That's what we use Fred's bicycles for. Ride them around and around and they can illuminate different puppets at different times."

"The songs can cross," Tonio said. "We use Persia's music hall idea, and she can make play lists the same way she's been making the Dau Hermanos menus. Each song should complement what came before and what comes after."

"I ride a bicycle very nicely, you know," said Max. He seemed to be talking to Nicholas while Tonio seemed to be answering questions I hadn't heard Floss ask. Lucia made new shapes with her fingers—bird, dog, elephant. Shadow puppets without the shadows.

"Could we get the audience to sing along?" Tonio asked.

"Depends on the songs," I said, "but it'd have to work at least part of the time."

"Because otherwise we have to have voice amplification."

"Megaphones?" said El Jeffery.

"As long as the lights travel, voice won't be that hard," said Nicholas.

"I'll do any puppet you want," said Lucia. "Two at once, even. But you all know I don't want to sing."

"'Mustang Sally' was damn good," Nicholas said.

Lucia blushed. "For you. Not for anyone else."

"We'll make it work," Tonio promised, and he wasn't just talking to Lucia. "We've got something exciting to play with now. Different. Fun. It can go in interesting directions."

"Back to that idea of audience participation," I said. "Backup singers for Lucia's puppets rather than strict karaoke?"

At that point every voice overlapped and all the words ran together like rainbow colors when the sky is wet and gray and the sun is just stumbling through. And just like that, snap, we were together again in a way we hadn't been since Major. Cohesion, some fun, "moralism without didacticism," and when I heard Floss say, "Mr. Fox is just like Major. Power in reviews compared to power in money," to El Jeffery I knew we were Outlaws again, too.

Tonio's Outline

Explication Interlude
Mr. Fox: A Puppet Show with Audience Participation

The general idea . . .

Elvira is a barely-making-it actress who's lured to quick money by Mr. Fox, a music hall producer. She thinks he's amazed by her talent. What he's really after is another person to add to his cluster of conquests. She doesn't know that he's a collector and that he uses his position to find the thing he most loves to collect—women—who sooner or later simply vanish. Gone forever. She's the sixth singer he's worked his magic on, but she'd never know that unless she tuned in to the backstage gossip, the rumors that say that all her predecessors have disappeared. But she won't listen. She's no gossipmonger.

Her new show starts out with the proverbial bang, but as it progresses she finds herself tied more and more to Mr. Fox. He controls her stage time, her rehearsal time, and her free time, all in the interest of "what's best" for her.

Elvira begins to feel grizzled, worn, with no chance or space to think for herself or to react to her circumstances. No matter which way she turns, he's there. Solicitous. Caring. Sinister.

She finally begins to listen to the backstage whispers. Several of the chorus singers are especially full of news. They knew previous lead singers three, four, and five. The more they tell her (through audience song choices from my play lists), the more Elvira believes that she's going to have to get herself away from this guy. And then she finds the boas.

Each singer has had a signature color. One night, just before she goes on, Elvira finds the yellow, pink, and green boas that match her red one. They're jammed in an obscure drawer in her dressing room. And now she realizes that she's going to have to do more than just get away. She's going to have to take Mr. Fox down. After all, she's not about to let herself join her disappeared predecessors. She's not about to get her boa stuffed in a drawer like a body part!

With the help of the chorus, Elvira concocts a secret finale that involves the whole cast and the audience in a rendition on that music hall favorite "That's What You Think." As they sing, the police that they've alerted storm the backstage and take Mr. Fox away. The last the audience sees of him, he's being led off stage left, draped in the boas of the previous singers.

"A morality play," El Jeffery said when he was filled in on the plot. "Just what we need."

XVII

"I need turquoise dinosaur fur."

The upstairs of Dau Hermanos looked much like it had when everyone had been trying to pull the first Mr. Fox together. But it felt completely different. There was a contentment in the air that was almost touchable, and a pleased but busy look on our faces.

Bron noticed. He came upstairs more and more often and peeked around doorjambs. I was alone, doing mock-ups for posters for the windows of the restaurant one afternoon when Bron actually came through the door instead of peeking into the room. He walked with the soft steps of a tired kitten.

"If I stayed here to watch, would I bother you?"

I shook my head.

"Because everyone else is very snippy when I try to get them to show me what they're working on." Then, as if he'd realized that he was picking on my playmates, he added, "Not that they shouldn't be. I guess putting a thing like this together is a little . . ."

"Insane," I supplied. "And each one of us goes through throes of importance at different times. Mostly it's just one or two at a time. Otherwise . . ."

"You'd kill one another?"

I laughed. "Probably. This way there's always at least one person to hold someone back."

"Do you make a pact?" Bron sat next to me on the wide, whitewashed floorboards. He sounded honestly interested. "You know, Persia can only be crazy when Tonio and Max are sane?"

"Nope." I grinned. "Just lucky, I guess."

Bron looked unconvinced, but all he said was, "Sing three?" His fingers floated above the words on my poster.

I sighed. "No, it's supposed to be read 'Sing Cubed.' I thought the number looked more dax, but now I wonder." I glared at the poster, then asked Bron, "What do you think?"

He tilted his head. "Cubed," he muttered. "Three. Times three. Oh! I get it. Sing, Sing, Sing, right?"

"If it's so obscure that it took that long, something's obviously wrong."

"No, no, not at all. I think that's good. Make them stop long enough to look at it, figure it out. It'll make them pay attention."

"You think? Because I could just use Mr. Fox."

"No." He dragged the word out. "Too much history here for that."

"The fairy-tale thing?"

"Right. You are, after all, in the land of magic, and that's where all those tales take place. Sometimes people ascribe bad connotations, which doesn't mean you shouldn't use it as a backdrop for the play, just that I wouldn't suggest it as your prime source of advertisement. Stick with 'Sing.' And stick with the word 'cubed.' If you use the word instead of the number, it's much more attention getting."

When Floss and Nicholas came in forty-five minutes

later we had a sign with a background of black washed to gray. The words were in golds and reds:

Sing Cubed!
IT'S FUN! IT'S FABULOUS!
It's Audience Participation Puppet Karaoke!

And we were in the middle of a debate about the angle of the smaller letters announcing dates and times. Since we were still deciding dates and times, this was more an exercise in layout design than anything else, but we were enjoying ourselves.

Nicholas leaned over my shoulder. His hand brushed against my hair. "Cubed?" he asked.

Bron held up three paint-splattered fingers.

"To the third power," Floss said. "Remember the name of this thing?"

Bron grinned and waved his three fingers in the air. Nicholas said the exact same thing Bron had said. "Of course! Tricky, but good. Make them think."

"See?" Bron said. "It works exactly the way we planned."

Floss nodded. "I like it." Then she turned to him and said, "I need turquoise dinosaur fur. Is Elbe still selling knickknacks and ephemera?"

Bron nodded. "He is. Fred said something about needing to go to Elbe's just this morning. I'm going to be busy soon with the early dinner folk. But if you and Fred go together, you know your chances of a direct hit will increase. Two are always better than one when Elbe is involved."

"Especially if one of the two is Fred," Floss agreed.

"This sounds interesting," Nicholas said. "Can I go too?"

"And me," I said, jumping up. "Anyone who sells dinosaur fur will most likely have something excellent that I really need. Or want."

"Only turquoise fur. No other colors," Floss cautioned me.

"That's okay." I patted her shoulder. "Fur colors aren't one of my major sources of interest."

"But light source is one of mine," said Nicholas. "Would this Elbe have anything I could use?"

Bron laughed. "Elbe has everything. It's getting to

him that's the problem. Taking Fred will help. He and Elbe have a bond."

As if he had been summoned, Fred walked into the discussion. "Actually, I've been wanting to see Elbe," he said, after Floss explained what she needed. "Now's as good a time as any." Nicholas and I followed Fred and Floss outside, and the Elbe search began.

Finding Elbe did take some time. Fred and Floss wandered in what seemed to be totally random patterns, passing each other now and then. Their mouths moved, but no discernible words came out. Nicholas and I started out trying to follow them, but it all became so complicated and convoluted that we finally gave up. We settled down on a bench in front of Dau Hermanos, and since I couldn't do anything but relax, that's just what I did. I was so relaxed it was almost shameful.

Floss walked past us, headed north. I watched her lazily, not turning my head, just letting her slide in and out of focus. Nicholas said, "It's good here. I like it."

"It seems safe, doesn't it? Warm. Easy. All that talk before about rulers and powers and dangers—it's like a book of myths."

"Do you miss it?" he asked suddenly. "Where we were before?"

I sat up straight, relaxation gone. "You sound like you think we're never going back." Even to myself, I sounded scared. Nicholas was right, it was good here, but I wasn't sure that I wanted to stay forever. Fred crossed behind Nicholas and bisected Floss's path. I tried to take the nervousness out of my voice and added, "They promised. We can still go home."

"Maybe we won't want to."

"Wait. Law school?"

He shrugged. "There must be some kind of fey court system. Maybe I'll talk to Fred or Bron." He looked past my shoulder, then switched his gaze to my face. He repeated, "It's good here, Persia. Being with you here is even better."

He looked at me for what seemed like a very long time and I forgot to worry about staying or going. I forgot to worry about anything except Nicholas. His eyes smiled, and when he moved to kiss me I was there before he was. It was a good kiss, a *B&B* kiss but better, because there was no acting required. They kept improving as we went along, these kisses. Very nice. Very promising.

When we broke apart Nicholas started to say something, but he never got the chance because behind us Floss said, "Ah," in a satisfied way. I looked over Nicholas's shoulder and, as if it had been there all along, a log building stood decked out in a wraparound porch, prayer flags hanging from the roof edges and fluttering in a nonexistent breeze. On the porch was an old-fashioned drink cooler flanked by two white rocking chairs. The word "Elbe" was written in blue on a board placed over the front door, and the whole place was framed by a perfect rainbow. I heard ice-cream truck music coming from inside.

"Hey," Floss yelled, in full stevedore voice. "Are you coming? Got to catch him while he's here."

By the time Nicholas and I got to the steps, Fred had disappeared inside and I could hear laughter. Floss slammed through the door. Nicholas and I walked with care, holding hands like Hansel and Gretel approaching the witch's cottage, but as soon as we were inside, I could tell that we didn't have one thing to worry about.

Elbe's was exactly like Knobbe's, and completely different at the same time. The atmosphere was Knobbe casual and Knobbe cluttered, but the stock was uniquely Faerie. I looked at the cauldrons and bolts of velvet, the arrows and the dried herbs, the shoes and the jars labeled "Wing Repair." I could see why Floss had wanted to come here for her dinosaur fur.

Fred was at the counter making a yellow and green wooden yo-yo do tricks that would have made a yo-yo professional sick with envy. He was barely watching his hands. Instead he was wrapped in deep conversation with a man who had Einstein hair the color of a blue Popsicle. He had one gold hoop on his left ear and two silver hoops on his right and a thick silver band on his right thumb. When Fred's yo-yo finally tangled in its string, he laughed like he'd heard the joke of the century.

"Practice, my man. Practice," he said, as Fred rolled the string back onto the toy. "You'll never get any good if you don't practice."

"So you say." Fred's voice was lazy and relaxed.

I didn't realize he'd heard us come in but, without turning around, he added, "These are our friends, Elbe. Persia, Nicholas, meet Elbe of Elbe's Old-Fashioned Emporium."

Elbe said, "Ah, part of Floss's group. Everyone's waiting for the show, you know. You're the talk of the neighborhood."

I glanced at Nicholas. "That's vaguely alarming."

"No, it's not," he said, and he grinned. "More like exciting."

"Exactly right," said Elbe.

"But we just finally got things organized enough to really think we could pull this off," I protested.

Elbe shrugged. "We're fey. We travel good news at a rapid rate."

"Nicholas needs lights," Fred said.

"Traveling lights. But I don't think I want candles," Nicholas added.

"Why not faerielight?" Elbe asked.

"I don't know much about it, and even if I did, I don't have any handy," said Fred. "But that might be an alternative." Their voices faded away as they walked to the back of the store.

I heard floorboards creak behind me. I turned and saw Floss walking toward the counter holding handfuls of turquoise fur. When she said, "Look! Perfect!" tips of the stuff got into her mouth.

I took a few pieces away from her. "You're going to choke on that," I said. The fur was soft, soft, and smelled like baby powder and fire.

Floss blew fur off her lips. "Thanks. Anything you need?"

I looked at all of it in pure delight and said, "How could I possibly know?"

Fred, Elbe, and Nicholas came back just then. Nicholas looked very pleased. He held a box that glowed with a soft, clear light around the edges, and Fred said, "I am buying this yo-yo. Very nice balance."

Floss put her fur down, and I added mine to her stack. "Seriously, Persia," she said. "If you want anything, get it now. Elbe never stays in one place for too long."

He sounded half apologetic when he said, "So many people need so many things."

"Bookmaking?" I asked. Elbe pointed to the far west wall. When I got there I breathed out, "Oh," on a long exhalation. The waxed threads alone were mind-boggling. They were arranged in careful rows following the color wheel, but every shade and tint was there too, not just normal color-wheel colors. Green, but not only light green, green, and dark green. There was willow, spring, frog, moss, fern, sage, olive—everything. Each color was like that. There must have been hundreds to choose from. I said, "Knobbe Three would be beside himself." If I'd had this before, those Dau Hermanos menus would have been unbelievable.

When Floss came up behind me and said, "Ready? Elbe has to be going," I was still simply standing and looking, on a color high.

"Persia?" Floss said, and she jiggled my arm.

"Not in a million years, Floss. I couldn't even start to be ready. Why didn't anyone tell me about this before I started those books for Bron?"

She lifted her shoulders. "I guess we never thought about it. It's Elbe. Everyone already knows."

"Not me. I didn't."

"You do now. Take what you want, and let's go."

"Floss, I can't," I moaned. "Just look at all of this."
I picked up a spool of cherry red with a brilliance that
said the cherries had just been picked from the tree
and turned into thread by fey magic. I waved it at
Floss and repeated, "Look!"

She sighed, a huge deep sound. "If you want something, you need to take it. Elbe has to go."

When I still stood there, just looking, she grabbed
two colors from each group. "I can use some of these
too," she said, and she caught my arm and walked me
up to Elbe.

Almost before I knew what had happened we were
standing in an empty spot near Dau Hermanos. Floss
held her armload of fur tied with a bright pink rib-
bon, Fred twirled his yo-yo, Nicholas held his box
of light and chewed on a peppermint stick as long as
his forearm, and I held a perfect package wrapped in
soft cream cloth with razor-sharp corners tied with a
jaunty, green striped bow.

"Wow," I said. "Talk about trippy."

Floss glanced at me over her pile of turquoise fur. "What? It's just Elbe." She shook her head and walked toward Bron and Rohan's. Fred followed her, his yo-yo walking behind him like a trained dog. Nicholas grinned. "Come on, Persia. Let's get my light upstairs. Then we can unroll your package and see exactly what Floss has decided you'll need." He looked down at me and jiggled his box of light. He sounded a little hesitant when he added, "Maybe we could work on that kiss a little more too. You know, that one we tried just before Elbe came?" He acted like he thought I might have forgotten.

"I didn't forget," I said, and I smiled at him. "Really."

He grinned himself, looked relieved, and nodded. "To get really good at something you have to practice. Just like the theater."

He was so sincere. I clutched my package a little tighter and leaned in to him. My lips touched his ear when I whispered, "Maybe we should just do the practicing now."

Nicholas stopped. Then he looked down at the

box in his hands, as if he'd just remembered he was holding it. With reluctance he said, "I need to get this inside." He shook his head. "I don't know anything about faerielight. Maybe it explodes if it's trapped for too long without air. Maybe it grows." He repeated, "Let me just get it upstairs."

I didn't think faerielight grew or exploded. Fred wouldn't let Nicholas handle growing or exploding stuff. But I was more than happy to follow Nicholas inside. Practicing your art was always important. And practicing kisses as art was even better. They were like chocolate, those kisses. Addictive.

XVIII

"You see underneath."

*W*e Outlaws were on a roll. Nicholas and Fred were concocting stilt platforms that would fit on our pilfered bicycles. Once they were finished, the platforms were going to be rigged to hold faerielights and gels. Floss was creating three-quarter life-size puppets dressed in lace, taffeta, ruffles, and fishnets. When I complimented her on her imagination she looked at her creations with a critical eye.

"Do you think so?" she asked. "I was worried that some of the people I'd modeled them on might take offense."

I looked at the nut brown pointed ears, at the gleaming teeth, at the seemingly lidless eyes, at the extra digit fingers. "You know people who look like this?" I asked. "Because even in the restaurant, I didn't notice anyone with those eyes." I looked again, more carefully this time, and added, "Some of the ears, maybe, but not those eyes. And certainly not those teeth."

She shrugged. "Persia. You haven't seen everyone, but I'm sure you've seen these. Maybe you're not paying attention."

I shook my head. "I'm paying attention, all right. I've seen Reginald, for example, and even though he's supercreepy—even he didn't have those teeth and those eyes."

Floss was working with tea-colored lace. She draped it around her neck, walked over to me, and searched my eyes. Then she shook her head. "There's no cloud over your eyes, Persia. You're seeing clearly."

She juggled the ends of her lace back and forth and seemed to be thinking. Then she said, "Maybe you're one of those who see the inside, not the outside." She looked at me again, and this time she nodded.

"Uh-huh. That's what it is, I think. It's your own form of magic." And she went back to crafting an elaborate ruched collar and tie for the shaggy turquoise dog made of Elbe's dinosaur fur.

I started to ask her to explain personal magic, and then I remembered it was Floss I was talking to. I might not understand, but if Floss said I had magic, it was probably true, at least on some level. It was also something I was going to have to figure out without her help because, again, this was Floss. She'd said what she thought. After that, she was usually through, no matter how much her comments left the other person in the dark.

I found Lucia involved in a deeply choreographed hand puppet chorus line, which isn't all that easy to do with hand puppets. Supplying her background music was Max, crooning dance-hall songs in a beautiful baritone. I watched for a minute. "Excellent," I said. "Quite dax. And this mixes with karaoke how?"

Max stopped singing. "Tonio's working out the final kinks in the dance-hall idea, so Lucia and I thought we'd work on the audience participation aspect. We handle the bigger puppets, and they get the small, less-important ones. They choose their song depending on the action."

I considered all the responses I could make and finally gave him the best one of all. "I like it."

"Of course you do," Tonio said, popping his head into the room. "The main idea was yours, after all. And that red you used for highlights on the posters is perfect for this. We just need to give everything that circusy, vaudeville look."

My mind ran with contrasting colors and design ideas. "Yes. Easy." I was almost out the door when I remembered what Floss had said. I repeated it. "Floss says I see the insides of things, not the outsides."

Lucia glanced up from the little earrings she was adjusting on her puppet's head. Without taking time to think she said, "You always have, ever since I've known you. You saw what I was right away."

"I saw a smart, sweet person who'd had a rough time," I said. "I saw a sparkle."

"Right. Most people saw a dirty, nasty street kid who was out to get them."

I stared at her in shock. "You?"

Lucia shrugged. "See?"

Tonio said, "The first time you saw me, Persia. Remember?"

"You gave me a paste pot and said that I looked open-minded."

"Yes, and you thought?"

Without considering I replied, "Kind. Gentle. Vaguely injured. Trustworthy."

Max grinned. "Perfect. Most people don't get past the first impression of gay."

"He was kind of flamboyant that day." I smiled. "But that's so superficial."

"What Floss said." Lucia's puppet nodded. "You see underneath."

"Well," I said. I'd have to think about this. I turned to go tackle my part of the preproduction, but I stopped in the doorway. "What's the final name of this, then?"

"Stay with *Sing Cubed*," Max said. "We thought we'd subtitle it *A Dance Hall Karaoke*."

I nodded. "Just so you know, Floss is making a blue

dog with a collar and tie."

"Darling," said Tonio, "you know Floss can make everything do anything."

He was right, of course. I nodded again and left to make vaudeville-themed programs. These would be my audience books for this production, but they'd be much more elaborate than my earlier books. Now that I'd had practice with Dau Hermanos's menus, I could fly with these books of lyrics. First the gray-and-black-washed covers with that red trim. Bindings stitched with those fabulous threads from Elbe's. Then all I'd need were the song lists. Maybe I could write the titles in gold and blood-red? Then they'd mimic the posters. When these programs passed through the crowd, they'd wow people. I was sure of it.

XIX

"Maybe he'll die."

$\mathcal{I}$'ve always liked to get up early. Less competition for thinking time and sitting time and staring into nothing time. It turned out that Bron had the same habit, so we'd come to the point of joint early-morning breakfasts. It was a little ritual of tea, sweet breads, and egg tacos. We'd sit in the early patches of sun that washed through the windows of Dau Hermanos. We wouldn't talk much, and when we did we'd just sort of throw words out and wait to see if they got caught. So it was something of a surprise when Bron addressed me directly just as I bit into a rolled tortilla. The other surprise was that he sounded hesitant, not like Bron at all.

"Persia," he said, and then his voice just faded away.

He shifted in his chair and looked at the bar instead of the window and tried again. "Persia."

I said, "Yes, Bron?" this time in an attempt to encourage him.

"There's something that may be a situation."

It took him a long time to say that sentence, and I felt a little chill run through the sunlight. "Maybe you just want to say it?"

He sighed a soft puff of air. "There's a rumor floating through the area. Reginald seems to have a houseguest."

Thankfully I could only imagine what living as Reginald's houseguest must entail. Just as I could only imagine what kind of a person would find a stay with Reginald attractive. "More power to the houseguest."

"Yes. Well. The particular houseguest seems to be a large part of the rumor. He's not fey. He crossed over without a guide so he must have a good deal of power."

"Lucia did it."

"Because she had a need, I imagine. She was hurt, after all. This visitor may or may not have been hurt when he came, but he does seem to have a tinge of helpful fey magic clinging to him."

"You just said he didn't have a guide."

Bron looked at me with wide eyes, then said, "A guide isn't at all the same as trace magic. You do know that, correct?"

"Actually, no, I don't know that. I also don't know if that's your point." I waited. When he didn't say anything else I asked, "So did Lucia have trace magic when she came?"

Bron shook his head. "Lucia didn't have the guide or the magic. I think she made a successful trip because of that trace of fey blood she carries."

I sat up straight. "Fey blood? Is that what gives her that sparkle when you look at her sideways?"

Bron eyed me with interest. "You see that?"

I nodded.

"Floss said you saw inside. Interesting. There aren't many of you."

I blushed. "I didn't even know there was one of me

till Floss said it. I'm still trying to figure out what it means. For example, does it mean I'm fey?"

Bron grinned. "Aren't we all?" he asked grandly.

"My parents would kill me if that was really true," I said.

"Not fans of Faerie, then?"

I laughed. "That's putting it so very mildly."

He laughed too. "Ah, well," he said, and he sounded vaguely rueful. Then he added, "Don't try to figure it out. Just let it be. It might mean you're part fey, it might mean you're sensitive, it might only mean you're highly perceptive. Worry about it too much and you might scare it away. Let's worry instead about Reginald's guest."

The chill crept back into the room, and I knew, just knew, what Bron was saying. "It's Major, isn't it?"

Bron watched me carefully as he said, "It's possible."

I growled. "He almost followed Floss once, and he's not happy with her because she doesn't appreciate his charms. Not that he has any, but still. He's furious angry with Tonio for jilting him and taking up with

242

Max. And those are just the reasons I know about for him to dislike us."

"So you think there are more?"

I wiggled my shoulders. "I'm sure there are, in his mind. Who knows how a brain like his works? Tonio says Major is power-mad. People like that can hate other people for almost anything. But Floss said a while ago that hate and anger weren't really good ways to get here. She said they were skinny emotions."

Bron held my eyes with his as he said in a careful voice, "Floss could be wrong in her assumption. Not about hate and anger in general—she's right about that. But there are factions that could find hate and anger very attractive. People who enjoy plying those particular emotions work easily with others who are like them."

It was obvious that I was being given a clue. "Reginald is in one of those factions, isn't he?"

"Reginald is . . . unpleasant. He's fascinated by Lucia. To put it mildly, he's not overly fond of Fred or me. We have a long history. He and Major would complement each other, I believe. And there are others in this corner of Faerie who might latch on to that hate and anger as well." He hesitated, then added, "Feron isn't overly fond of his younger brother, or of me, either. And Feron and Floss have never gotten along."

"Fred said Feron wasn't around."

"There are different ways of being around," Bron said, which I thought was a slanted comment.

"Just when things were getting really good again." I don't think I was talking to Bron right then. I was just talking. "And Tonio. Damn, he was finally starting to really look like Tonio again. And Nicholas is so happy trying to understand those faerielights. Floss is building blue dogs. Lucia is playful, and Max—Max is singing!"

"Things are rarely perfect, and if they are it's not for long. And you knew that there was danger in Faerie, just as there is in your world. Major, if it is Major, is only a part of that."

I waved my hand, brushing aside the idea of fey danger. "I know, you said. Everyone said. Floss especially. But there hasn't been much sign of it." I sighed, then glanced sideways at him and, slightly embarrassed, said, "I wanted to believe it was all sunshine and flowers."

Bron snorted. "You see inside things. Don't expect me to believe you didn't see danger."

"Little things. That blood smell when we came through. Creepy Reginald, and if I really do see inside things, I don't see any difference between the inside and the outside of him. That aura that surrounds you and Fred sometimes."

"You saw that? I thought we had that under wraps."

I opened my eyes wide. He shrugged. "It's mostly just something that happens when there's someone close by that we have bad feelings about. Reginald brings it out in spades."

"More information?" I asked, when he didn't offer anything else.

"No more. It just pays to be wary. Exactly like in your world."

I waited, but it seemed like that was all I was going to get. I said, "You know, I wanted it to be safe here. I wanted it to be better than home. I wanted us to be happy."

"But aren't you? Right now, at this time, in this place, aren't you?"

"I was," I said, emphasis on the past tense. "Why can't Major just quit?"

"I suppose he gets some points for stick-to-itiveness."

I growled again. "He gets no points. Never, never, ever." Then I brightened. "If it was hard to get through, maybe he's hurt. Maybe he'll die." I sounded like an eight-year-old wishing revenge, but I didn't care. I widened my eyes at Bron and waited for some kind of confirmation.

Floss said, "Who's going to die? Besides me, I mean, if I don't get coffee and something to eat." She filled a huge mug from a tiny silver pot and snatched two tacos from the warming tray. She drenched the tacos with enough hot salsa to last me a solid week, then dropped down at our table. After finishing one taco in three bites she swallowed a big gulp of coffee and repeated, "Who's going to die?"

"Probably no one." I sounded morose. "Probably it's just wishful thinking on my part."

Floss seemed surprised when she said, "Death wishes. Not your normal thing, Persia, unless of course you were talking about Major, who'd deserve it. Or at times my older brother. But since Major's not here, and Feron seems to be out of the area too, I don't . . ."

She stopped like she'd run into a wall. "Major's here." It wasn't a question. "If you're talking about it"—and she looked at me—"it has to be Major. You'd never know if Feron was around."

"From your previous description, Major seems to be a good guess," Bron said in a toneless voice. "I couldn't say about Feron."

Floss devoured her second taco, finished her coffee, put both elbows on the table, dropped her head into her hands, and said, "Major. I should have paid more attention. Oh, fuck."

"I heard that." Tonio spoke quietly. "And I'm not talking about the swearing. Floss, whatever's going on isn't your fault."

Floss just sighed, a deep, mournful sound that came from her boots.

"Maybe he'll just die," I tried again. "Or better, be

so hurt he'll leave and never try again."

Tonio stepped in front of me, tilted his head, and said, "That doesn't even make sense."

I said, "Bah."

Tonio shook his head. "I understand the sentiment, but we have to at least make logical sense. It's a requisite for humanity. If he were that hurt, how could he move?"

"Bah," I repeated, but this time I wasn't disgusted. Tonio wasn't in panic mode. He wasn't in despair, either, which would have been worse. He was just Tonio, which made me feel that the morning had just taken a giant step toward improvement.

El Jeffery and Fred came in just as the rest of the Outlaws clattered down the stairs. And because Tonio wasn't despairing, once everyone was up-to-date our discussion seemed more of a chat or an intellectual exercise than anything else. I relaxed and even Floss began to seem a little less guarded.

"It's still only a rumor, after all," El Jeffery said. "And rumors flow around here like marsh water after a long rain." It was many cups of coffee later, and we were all looking well-fed and a little lazy. Everyone nodded.

Then Rohan came in. He motioned Bron to the other side of the room, the side by the kitchen door. Everyone tensed again. I felt it and I started a new ride on the roller coaster of bad news. Because, really, why would Rohan be whispering if he had good news?

Bron came back to the table, and Rohan came with him, his face grim. "Rohan has a cousin," Bron began, "who often walks through Reginald's land. He reports a flurry of activity lately, something easy to notice. Reginald is generally very low-key, and low movement. And the cousin reports a dark-haired human, badly injured."

"No magic or fey blood about him," added Rohan. "It's hard to hide what you truly are when your strength is gone. But there is definitely some kind of Faerie assistance running with him, and it doesn't feel like it belongs to Reginald."

Floss sat up straighter. "Feron?" she asked. "He's just the kind to help someone like Major, although Mab knows how they would have met. But if they had met, they'd match each other perfectly. And Feron and Reginald have always had some kind of strange connection."

"Nastiness attracts?" Fred asked.

"Of course it does," said Bron. "But all the other things we've put together are guesses. Except, of course, for the fact that Reginald's guest is a mortal."

Rohan added. "And if he associates with Reginald, we can assume he's an unpleasant or dangerous one. Right now he seems to spend most days sitting near the river in the sun. I believe your guess as to his identity is correct, though. One afternoon my cousin heard Reginald call him Major."

There was one of those long seconds of silence. Then Floss shook her head hard, hard enough to make her hair fall into her eyes. I thought I heard it swish in the breeze. She looked straight at Tonio and said, "So we were right. Oh, Tonio, I'm so sorry. I got all caught up in the play. I was at home. I felt safe." She paused and then, shoulders slumped, she added, "I should have known better."

Tonio rubbed Floss's left hand. He was almost

casual when he said, "I told you before. Nothing that's happened is your fault."

"But I was supposed to be the fey guide. I was——"

Tonio interrupted her. "Floss. Really. We all knew there were risks. They're all around us—all around everyone, really. Every day. Drop it."

Floss sighed one more time. The glance she slid toward Tonio held that Floss–Tonio bond. He saw it, and his lips curved in a small, quirked smile. Floss sat up straight and gave him a sheepish half-grin back.

When she spoke again, sounding more like herself, she only said, "I just wish I knew who helped him. This is all too coincidental—we come here, Major comes here, and Feron isn't in evidence. Major's living at Reginald's; Reginald and Feron have always seemed to think alike." She hesitated, then finished with "It's all so random that it shouldn't mesh at all, and those are usually the things that are most true. Fred, is your Feron radar better than mine?"

Fred shrugged. "I haven't been able to tell a damn thing about him since I was six."

"That part's all guesswork anyway," Tonio said, waving the idea of Feron away. "For now we'll just consider Major."

Confirmation is an interesting thing. Now that we all knew, knew for sure that we had Major in our lives again, there was almost a sense of relief. It was as if we'd been waiting without knowing what we were waiting for.

"Maybe," Max mused, "it's dealing with the familiar."

Floss made a low noise deep in her throat.

"I know, I know," Max said. "But everything's been turned upside down since we came here." He looked at Floss and amended, "Well, for most of us. In some weird way this kind of puts us back on level ground."

"Right," Nicholas said. "Not good ground, but level ground."

Lucia, though, looked stricken. She shook her head. "It's too rocky to be level. Major. Reginald. Maybe your brother, Floss. Sometimes even the magic is hard." She looked like she was going to cry. "It's too much stuff. Too much to deal with."

I remembered her chorus line, how happy she'd seemed. Max singing. Tonio relaxed and working. All of us adjusting. And I found that I didn't want to be on familiar ground if it meant giving up our happiness and independence and that good little flutter in your stomach that came when you skipped into the unknown. It made me mad, this Major appearance.

I said, "He doesn't have a right to ruin our lives. Or to run our lives. And there's still that chance that he'll just keel over and die."

"Hear, hear!" El Jeffery waved his arm in the air, which made Floss giggle.

"But even if he doesn't—oh, hell," I said. "We didn't let Reginald ruin everything when we first came here, and he's been in the background all along. We just did what we do."

"Even before, when we were doing *The Bastard and the Beauty*, we didn't let Major stop us," Nicholas added. "At least not until he proved he was dangerous, and then we adjusted."

"True. Right. Past experiences color the present,

but the colors aren't perfect. They can shade or tint," Max said.

"Or wash away, like chalk in a rainstorm." Lucia, looking more like Lucia, grinned, seeming pleased with her analogy.

Floss stood up, chattering her chair legs. "Persia's right. There's no point spending all your time fighting when you don't even know if you need to fight. I've got work to do."

Tonio followed her, striding out of the room and saying, "You can only prepare if you know what to prepare for. I've got a play to build."

Max smiled and followed Tonio. Nicholas laughed. "Now look what you've started, Persia. Puppet revolution."

"Not me," I protested. "It's been here ever since we came up with a solid idea for the Mr. Fox story. After all, that's a definite poke and prod. Very revolutionary."

That made Lucia perk up. "We are the Outlaws, after all." Then, as if everything was settled, she let her thinking take a right turn and said, "And Fred, you did say something about actually understanding the inner workings of a slide rule, didn't you? Max is fretting about box office accounting."

"I understand them. I just don't have one. But I think we can find Elbe. He's sure to have at least six different types, in various colors." Fred swirled his yo-yo in the streams of sun, and it flashed the color of wet stones on the beach. Then he held out his hand. Lucia took it with a familiarity I hadn't seen before, and they walked together out of Dau Hermanos.

Nicholas watched them leave. "Nice," he said. Then he reached in his turn for my hand and said, "So. You want to help with the faerielights? I seem to have lost my work partner."

I snuggled my hand in his. Warm, long fingers with a tiny callus on his left hand, probably from all those hours of writing law briefs. Nice, indeed.

"I'll help," I said, "if you'll help with the paint finishes on the posters. Fred was working on that, too."

Bron chuckled. "Fred. He's more of an outlaw than he'd ever have you believe. Sometimes I think he's more subversive than Floss. It's just a different kind of subversion. Much more indirect." He glanced after Floss with a fond expression and added, "Floss is so in-your-face. I like that." He nodded. "I think she might need help with that blue dog."

"Go, go." Rohan shooed him away. "I'll call you when the rush starts."

Nicholas and I followed Bron. Pairs, I thought, pleased. Bron and Floss. Fred and Lucia. Max and Tonio. Nicholas and me. Nice. And to hell with Major.

"It must be all that residual magic Floss talked about. She said it could energize. Everything seems fine right now," I said.

Nicholas squeezed my hand and kissed the top of my left ear. I cuddled into him and dropped my hand in his back pants pocket. Muscles moved when he walked, like words linking together into pieces of poetry. He glanced down at me and grinned. "I like that," he said. "You should put your hand on my butt more often."

I laughed, but he just kept walking and talking. "I agree with you, though. Everything feels fine. I know Major's here, but what can he do? Even with

Reginald, he can't have the power he had at home. This is Faerie, after all. He's out of his element. Reginald's been an unpleasant thought, but not dangerous and not even around except for that one time. Major hasn't announced himself." He shrugged. "We'll be fine, right?"

"Of course," I said. "Why not?"

XX

"Karaoke isn't quite the family style."

*R*emember this, I was thinking to myself. If something happens, if everything else goes south, remember this.

It was a night cool enough to wear sweatshirts and warm enough to sit outside, which is exactly what Nicholas and I were doing. The breeze was light. The stars were out, and in Faerie that's a sight beyond compare. I saw more stars that night than I'd seen in all my years added together. And there were twilight fireflies blinking secret messages to one another that added even more atmosphere.

"Wish I knew what they were saying."

"That's easy," Nicholas said. "They're saying, 'I'm

here. I'm one of a kind. I'm beautiful.' Like what you say, Persia."

I sat up straight and stared at him through the darkness. "What are you talking about? I don't say anything like that at all."

He swung an arm around my shoulders. When he talked I could feel his breath on my hair. "There's a uniqueness to you that just comes through. It's in the way you talk, the words you choose, the way your right foot makes a little curve when you walk. It's the clothes you wear and the jewelry you don't. It all adds up and makes a neat little Persia package that's just . . ." He paused and pulled back just a bit. ". . . just you." He kissed me then, a lovely, long kiss. Practice makes perfect. When we stopped he added, "I like it."

I was breathless and I felt as floaty as one of Floss's pink clouds. But he had everything upside down. "You've got it all wrong," I whispered. "You're the firefly one. There's not one thing special about me."

"You don't think so?"

I shook my head.

"That makes you even better."

I blew out a puff of air and said, "I'm glad you like it, anyway. Like me." I felt shy now, because it's always hard to talk about honest, serious things. But I did it anyway when I added, "Really glad. Which sounds inadequate and juvenile, and that's not at all how I feel."

It was a good thing that it was dark. It's easier to talk in the dark. Nicholas apparently thought so too. "Maybe we should try something like that kiss again. You know, just to make absolutely sure we're compatible," he said.

I pulled back after several long minutes where there seemed to be nothing in my head but happiness and tried to see his face in the firefly light. I couldn't see much. The fireflies were too busy with their own lives to shine much light on mine. But that was okay. I didn't really need to see. I could feel. And what I felt was warm and solid and true.

"At some point," I said carefully, "would you be interested in taking this . . . further?"

He smiled. Even in the dim light I could tell that.

"I would be"—he kissed my nose—"very interested. Do you suppose we can find a quiet place and a free bit of time?"

I considered what I knew about Faerie and quiet, secret spaces while I tucked myself in under Nicholas's arm. I pulled that arm around me, wrapped myself in it like a cloak of warmth and power. And I said, "Fred and Bron probably know lots of cozy, empty spaces where—"

As if we'd summoned him. Fred interrupted me by saying, "Sorry to interrupt." He came out of the night surrounded by fireflies glowing like hundreds of tiny lanterns. "Thank you," he said to them, and the fireflies bobbed air curtsies and flew away. Fred stopped in front of Nicholas and me. He stopped, and suddenly the night felt airless and tinged with menace. He dropped onto the bench next to me and said, "I'll just sit, if you don't mind." His voice was as flat and thin as the air, and the bench shook when he landed.

Nicholas shifted and peered around me. "What's up?"

Fred took a deep breath. "If I say treachery at the

261

crossroads, would you believe me?"

"I'd get the idea, I think," Nicholas said, "but I'd have to ask you to be a little more specific."

I could feel Fred lean his head against the wall of Dau Hermanos. It was a hard lean. "How do you suppose factions come together?"

"There are factions?" I asked while Nicholas said, "Is this rhetorical?"

Fred answered him, not me. "Not rhetorical at all. How does one decide who to align with, after all?"

"Same ideas, same plans, same desired end," I suggested.

"I suppose." Fred sighed. "I was at home, you know. Just at that place where Floss says she'll never go again and with some very good reasons. I was at home. El Jeffery and I were working on a drum piece he wants to use because he's convinced he's to be in the play."

"He is," I confirmed. "Lucia wants him to sing, as well."

Fred's head shake was just visible. "Don't let him. He's never been able to sing."

"He's in the band, right?"

262

"Drums, Persia, only drums. He's definitely not solo singing material."

"I think she meant backup," Nicholas said, "but never mind. You were working on a drum piece and . . . ?"

"We were in the storage areas because he insisted he had to ride while playing. For verisimilitude. We were making quite a racket, so when we stopped, all the sounds we'd been covering up were magnified. And even though Reginald walks very softly for a troll, he still makes noise."

"Reginald?" Nicholas sounded both unhappy and disapproving.

"He apparently has much better relations with my parents than my sister has. Perhaps good relations with my brother, as well. At least, he didn't look scared or cowed on his way to the manor."

"Reginald is visiting your house?"

"Was he alone?" I added.

"Yes, he was visiting my house. Yes, he was alone. Yes to both is better than yes and no, but no to both would be better still."

I was angry with this news from Fred. It showed when I said, "Why does it feel like everyone around here speaks in riddles?"

"Do we?" It was almost an abstract question. Fred shifted on the bench. "I suppose it's just our way."

"It makes things that much harder, you know," I said.

Nicholas ignored me and cut to the important part. "Do we need a war council?"

"We at least need to let the others know that something's going on," said Fred.

I sighed a deep, heavy sigh. I stood up, and I held on to Nicholas's hand while I did it. "Life is just full of ups and downs, isn't it?" I pulled the memory of earlier in the evening a little closer, like a talisman.

Nicholas tightened his grip on my fingers. "Sure it is. We just need to keep the ups higher up, so to speak."

"Yes. Let's try that," Fred said, but he didn't sound very hopeful.

It was late enough that most of the Dau Hermanos customers were gone, and those that remained were sitting at the bar, paying no attention to us. Nicholas went to gather the rest of the Outlaws while Fred told Bron and Rohan what he'd seen. I stood at a table large enough for all of us, shoving chairs in and pulling them out again while I tried to pretend that I was doing something useful. It was both too late and too soon when everyone else began to drift into the room.

Floss looked like daggers were sprouting from her shoulder. Lucia looked sad. Tonio and Max were enigmatic—I couldn't read them at all. Bron sat next to Fred and didn't say a thing until Rohan brought a jug of sangria to the table, accompanied by dried currents and tiny shortbreads. Even then, all Bron said was "Thank you," and he sounded like he was pushing a remote to make the words.

El Jeffery shoved through the door and squished in next to Lucia. "Reginald just left. He's headed toward home. And yes," he said as he looked at Fred, "he's still alone. And no, I didn't see anyone walking him to the gate. Like your brother or your mother, for example. Or your father."

Fred shook his head. "Father would be the least

likely of anyone to walk to the gate with him. He does have *some* standards."

"If he'd just exercise them every now and then . . . ," Floss muttered, and she left the sentence unfinished.

Silence. Then Tonio said, "I don't think I like the idea of Reginald having little chats with the ruling family." I considered this to be a grand understatement.

Floss tapped her nails in staccato on the table. She said, "I am so thoroughly tired of other people interfering in my life." She glanced around the table and corrected herself. "In our lives."

"Maybe he was delivering a gift. A fruit basket, a bouquet," said Max, and to my surprise Tonio laughed.

Even I smiled. "The image of that is so surreal. I kind of like it."

"Glad to help," Max said.

Fred took a gulp of sangria and said, "I didn't even know he knew our family."

"He may not." I tried the idea to see how it sounded in the open air. "This may be the first time he's ever been there. You know, subject visiting ruler . . ."

Floss glared at me. "No, Persia. Nice try, but no. If he's going somewhere this late, he has business at the destination."

I tried again. "But—"

"I said no." Floss's voice was mild. "Trolls always prefer daylight. They think that if people can really see them it makes them scarier."

"They might be right," I half whispered.

El Jeffery ignored us both. "He looked pleased with himself."

"Has anyone heard more about Major?" Tonio asked. He wasn't, I was happy to see, the Tonio of the days before we'd walked out the back of the chocolate factory. He was the old Tonio, the one who knew just who he was and what he wanted. "Because if Reginald is his shill—and in a pairing of those two I can't imagine things going any other way—then he's really only the errand boy."

"I can't believe that Reginald runs the thing, whatever the thing is," Bron agreed.

Lucia said, "Maybe there is no thing." She looked at Fred, hope in her eyes, but he just patted her hand.

"Brave but delusional, I think," he said, and he gave her a glass of wine. Lucia breathed out a lengthy breath, sank back into her chair, and took a long drink.

"I can ask around," Fred went on, "but I think if your Major's involved . . ."

"And in spite of the fruit basket comment, I'm sure he is," Max said with a sigh.

Fred nodded. "Is it better to just go and ask him?"

"Catch the lion in his lair?" I asked.

"If Major's involved, he's not running things," Floss said flatly. "We can ask him all we want, but he's not the one in charge. Not here. He might be running Reginald, but he's not running anything else. It's much more likely, if the family's involved, to be either our mother or our brother."

Fred sighed and beat a tattoo on the table with his fingertips.

"You don't agree?" Floss asked him.

Fred looked surprised. "Of course I agree."

Floss looked pointedly at his fingers, still tapping the table.

He half smiled. "Nerves, not disagreement," he said.

Max sighed, and a piece of paper fluttered down in front of him as if he'd asked for it. Max looked at it, inches from his fingertips, and he didn't move at all. It was Tonio who picked the thing up and unwound its complicated, origami-like folds.

Tonio read, and the rest of us sat and watched until Max said, sotto voce, "I hate to say this, but he has more of a sense of style than I've given him credit for."

"Who?" I whispered.

"Major. Or whoever he's playing with. It's got to have something to do with him. The timing is just too perfect. This is really quite good theater."

Floss snorted. "So someone floated a letter. Anyone can float a letter."

"Um, no Floss, they can't," Nicholas said.

Floss snorted again, and Max said, "The float was the least of it, I think."

Tonio looked up. "Major seems to be feeling better. His emissary"—tiny finger quotes—"has met with Floss and Fred's family. Major believes that the Outlaws have entered Faerie illegally. . . ."

"There's a legal way to get here?" asked Nicholas.

"That's interesting." He turned to Fred. "Is that true? Did we need passports or something?"

Fred's snort sounded exactly like his sister's. "If you're not fey, you get here any way you can. There's no legality involved. Either you make it or you don't."

"So he's building a false case."

Tonio coughed. "May I continue? There's more. Perhaps before we debate legal and illegal you'd like to hear the whole thing?"

"Of course we would," Max said, and he rubbed Tonio's shoulder.

Tonio nodded. ". . . have entered Faerie illegally. Rather than forcibly ejecting us the royal family will allow us to perform for them. The worthiness of our show will be the determining factor on whether we're allowed to stay. Conversely, if we don't meet expectations, we'll be banished from Faerie forever." Here he let his gaze brush Floss, Fred, and El Jeffery. "All of us, banished forever."

The implications were transparent. Floss, at the very least, could lose any chance of ever returning again to the land of her birth. And if the rest of us were tossed away, Major could follow us back home and start the whole mess all over again. Banishment here. Who-knew-what waiting for us there. Major very possibly able to bounce over to either side. Sort of the rock-and-the-hard-place scenario.

"Who writes his dialogue?" I sounded peevish because I was scared. "'Banished forever.' If we did a play that sounded that stilted, we'd deserve to be booed off the stage."

Floss cast her scowl in my direction. "True, Persia, but not even one tiny bit helpful."

I shrugged. "I'm just saying."

"I don't think the dialogue's the important part." Tonio looked at Floss and said, "After everything you've told me about your home, I have a hard time believing your family will rave about puppets. I think they'll be even less excited about puppet karaoke that seems to be criticizing their rule."

"I haven't even told you all that much," Floss said. "And it *is* criticizing their rule."

"So you agree with me?"

"Mab, Tonio, of course I agree with you," Floss

said. "Aside from the very obvious fact that we're not ready. . . ."

"Does it say when?" Max asked. "When this preview is supposed to take place?"

Tonio looked at the letter again, but I had the feeling that he already knew the answer. "In two days' time," he said.

"Oh, please," I said, while Lucia whispered, "Two days?" and Nicholas said, "I have to say that I, personally, am not ready. I don't have even one faerielight that works the way it should. And what I don't have doesn't even begin to cover us as a group, or to mention all the other ways that we're not prepared."

"Add in the fact that we still don't have a real script, just an outline concept," said Tonio.

"It's impossible," I said.

"Yes, well, it's my parents," Floss said viciously.

"Oh, I'm sure Major had some say," Max said.

"But can you do it?" Fred added, "I don't understand half of what you all do. Can you do it?"

Bron passed the sangria. I pulled a slice of orange out of my glass and chewed on it. "No."

"Persia, you're usually positive," Lucia cried.

I slumped in my chair and stared at her. "I know, I know. But two days? Lucia, we don't have—anything!"

"We do, though," Max said suddenly. Everyone turned to look at him. "We have an idea and a name. I know Floss has puppets we can use because, as Tonio says, Floss can make everything do anything. Nicholas at least has an idea for a light source. Persia has signs. Tonio has an idea, and if we can't improv with one another after this long, what's the point?"

"We won't have polish, that's for sure," Tonio said, "but we do have a little bit of something."

"We have karaoke. We have audience sing-along." Floss looked at us each in turn. "I can guarantee my family will not enjoy or participate in karaoke or something that resembles a hootenanny."

"Floss would be right about that." Fred sounded apologetic. "Karaoke isn't quite the family style."

While Floss muttered, "Our family has no style. Of any kind," I said, "So we treat it like a rehearsal and cross our fingers and hope?" The two sentences twisted around each other and came out sounding like "Our family treats it like a rehearsal—no style and hope."

Fred blinked. "That was interesting. It just blended so well. Can you do that in a play?"

Floss and I sat up straight. We grinned at each other. "You know," I said, but Lucia beat me to it.

"Blended audience participation dialogue," she said gleefully. "They feed us lines based on the song lyrics. . . ."

"And we pull the play along with the songs themselves," I finished.

Lucia nodded. "Like Max said. Improv." She took a deep breath and added, "I'll even sing."

Nicholas and Floss both looked at her, eyes wide, and said, "Lucia! Yes!"

"We still have to have lyrics to pick from," Max said, talking over them, "but we can come up with some select choices for Persia's books. We can pick things that can help us get where we want to go, one way or another."

"We'll just use the basic plot from the outline I started the day we decided to switch to the dance-hall scenario. We all know Mr. Fox, so we should be able to work with that easily enough," Tonio said.

"They won't participate. You know that, right?" Fred asked, his eyes on Floss.

Floss's nostrils flared as she breathed in. She finally said, "Maybe some of the staff will be there."

Fred looked at her as if she were delusional, and Floss shrugged.

"Then we throw out the line ourselves and go from there." She sounded quite determined.

Max turned to Nicholas. "We can get enough light with candles if we have to. We just can't move much."

Nicholas nodded. "Right. Candles definitely won't work on the bikes, but I'm sure Fred can help me get a least one faerielight platform and the light that goes with it ready to go."

Fred said, "Possibly," but he didn't sound like he was thinking about his answer. He seemed hesitant when he added, "You were in the depths of despair, and now . . ."

"Now," Floss said to her brother, "we have something to work with." She sent him a subversive, little grin and added, "And we *will* make it work."

"It turns that fast?"

Floss shrugged. "Sometimes."

"Just give me a beat," El Jeffery said. "You'll have background."

Tonio smacked the table with his palms in 4/4 time. "I'll find songs that match."

Floss was counting on her fingers. "With the blue dog we have six workable puppets." She paused, then said, "They still won't like it, you know."

"Ah," I said, "but maybe they won't hate it. That gives us a lot of wiggle room."

XXI

"You've just never seen my feet."

*T*wo days is a very short time. Things that get accomplished in two days may include, but are not limited to, the following:

> *Even if you're doing improv there's no space for improv*
> *in anything technical, so you spend a lot of time*
> *on backstage magic.*
> *You work with what you have and don't whine about*
> *what you don't have.*
> *Lots of wonderful ideas get tabled because there's just*
> *no time to work them in.*
> *You become highly creative.*
> *You get angry with everyone and try to pretend you're*

not angry at all.

You get very little sleep, and it begins to show.

You put together a lyrics list full of short lines that can mix and match, cross your fingers, and think good thoughts whenever possible.

All things taken as equal, I thought we were doing fine. Our songs had been picked by Tonio, and he'd done a brilliant job, choosing old dance-hall and vaudeville tunes that at least one or two of us knew and that the rest of us could background. Then he and I pulled the best lines and came up with an eclectic list of eighteen short sentences. I'd made as many sample books as I could using materials from Elbe's, and they looked, even if I was the one to say it, brilliant. Bindings worked with that gorgeous cherry red thread twisted together with a deep sea blue. Water-washed black covers fading to those myriad shades of gray that Fred and I had worked on. Cream parchment inside with filigree lettering in blood and gold. The whole package looked like a carousel.

Floss's blue dog was the obvious evil star of this

production. We'd all decided he was our best bet for Mr. Fox. Now, along with his lace collar and tie, he had a bowler hat. This shouldn't have come close to working, but it did. Even with his blue-tinged fur he made a believable producer. Lucia made him move so convincingly that he had to have a name. We came up with Edgar, which made us all start referring to the whole enterprise as Edgar Fox's Downfall.

"Downfall," Floss said, and she was fierce. "Let's plan on it being theirs, not ours."

Almost as an afterthought she added, "And not Fred's either. Poor thing. He's more or less stuck right in the middle. And he's not really doing anything that they could hate."

"Of course he is," I pointed out. "He's doing all that work with Nicholas."

Floss said a noncommittal, "Hmm."

"Ah, maybe you're right," I said. "It's just lighting, after all. Who could hate lighting?"

That was the exact moment we heard a loud "Damn" from next door. Then we heard rapid footsteps, so we peeked into the hall. Both Fred and

Nicholas were there, and they looked nervous. There was a scent of burning in the air, a large hole in Nicholas's shirt, and a smudge on Fred's left hand, just above the silver band on his first finger.

"Faerielight," Fred muttered, "is not supposed to act like that. It's supposed to be well behaved at least, even if it doesn't do exactly what you want it to do."

"Whatever," Nicholas said. "It's acting like that, and it seems to want to keep acting like that. Let's just forget the flash. We don't need the flash. At least not enough to risk burning down the stage."

Fred opened the door to their workroom with caution. "It's fine now. It's out."

"No flash," Nicholas repeated, as if to convince himself, and they went back inside.

Floss and I had barely moved back to our own projects when Lucia, Max, and Tonio walked past our door arguing. "If we don't stage it with a dance-hall proscenium, why are we even bothering?" Lucia asked. She had a sock puppet with long black curls, tiny gloves, a miniature red bustier, and a flowing red feather boa. The puppet looked very dance hall, which was impressive, because it's hard to do a lot of costuming with a sock. Hard to accessorize, too, apparently. Her earrings looked like two teeny, twisted paper clips.

"We don't have time to make a proscenium," Max said, which I thought was pretty realistic. "Especially not one with red and gold curtains."

"Cardboard?" Lucia tried. "Or some kind of puppet?"

"No more puppets. I don't have time," Floss yelled into the hall in her stevedore voice.

"And it will be on a stage," Tonio promised. "We'll create the illusion."

"Sometimes," Lucia's puppet muttered as they banged down the stairs, "illusion is harder than reality."

"How true," Floss said. "But I really don't have the time to make reality. And I need enough green tulle to make three small ballet skirts."

Before I could say anything, she added, "For the chorus line."

"We have a chorus line?" I asked.

Floss sighed. "Of course not, Persia. I can only do so much. We have six-fingered minikin rod puppets who dance in the background. They're attached to one another so we only need one person to move the whole group. That's why the skirts have to be so small. I wish I knew where Elbe was."

Although this series of sentences lacked Floss's usual polish and flow, I got the idea. "I'll go look for Elbe," I volunteered.

She shook her head. "That would be useful, but you'll never find him alone. You need a guide." She thought for a minute, then said, "Take El Jeffery."

"He won't go," I said. "He says his drums aren't ready. Surely you've heard all the noise? It's been like a backdrop to every conversation for hours now."

"Oh, I've heard," Floss said. "If he's not willing to go, if he says he needs more practice, tell him he's got his drums close enough to perfection. Convince him that he'll lose his edge if he keeps banging away at them, that he won't be any good tonight."

"Okay. I can but try. And when I come back I can do a sketchy stage opening. I'm done with the song lists."

"Fine. Tell Lucia on your way out. She'll stop worrying. I need a relaxed dog tonight."

When I found El Jeffery he was slouching through Dau Hermanos smacking a marching band drum. All the racket was making Bron and Rohan roll their eyes and exhale long, heavy breaths.

"He fluctuates between being puffed up and full of himself because he's to be in the play, and looking vaguely ill because he's to be in the play," Bron said, speaking louder than he normally would. I knew he was trying to be heard over the drum, but I also thought he might be sending a message to the griffin. When he added, "And of course, there's the banging," I was sure about the message.

I went over to El Jeffery and said, "You're going to be wonderful. Think of this as a dress rehearsal, instead of something important." His eyes got big when I said important, so I hurried to add, "And I really need you to help me."

El Jeffery perked up and put his drumsticks down. He seemed pleased to have a distraction. "Of course, Persia. What can I do?"

"We need to find Elbe. Floss needs green tulle, and she says I'll never be able to find him by myself."

"This is true," he said. "Elbe rarely lets himself be found by someone who isn't Faerie-born." He led the way outside and we began the complicated to-ing and fro-ing that was involved in tracking Elbe's store. This time I followed in his tracks. It didn't help. I still had no hint of what we were doing, and I knew I'd never be able to replicate these pseudo—dance steps on my own.

But El Jeffery was good. We were on Elbe's porch in just under ten minutes, caught in the glow of colored lights coming through the rainbow that seemed to be one of Elbe's permanent fixtures. When I complimented the griffin he said, "Only because he wanted us to find him."

"Wouldn't he always?" I asked. "He sells stuff."

"Depends on who's looking, and for what," El Jeffery said obliquely.

We found what I considered the right tulle for Floss's job and took it to the counter.

"Big show tonight," said Elbe.

"Word travels," said El Jeffery.

For some reason those five words sparked my idea. From the start I'd had more nervousness about going to Floss's family's house than about anything else. It seemed like we were walking in with the odds stacked against us. But . . . "Elbe," I cried, "could we do the show here? We could stage off the porch. It's even got semi—side wings. And you've got controllable lights and a place for puppets to come and go."

Elbe squinted his eyes. "The lights only work inside."

"That's okay. I think they've got the stage lights figured out." While this wasn't even partially true, it made me sound confident. "But we could use back-stage lights, too."

He wiggled his shoulders. "I'm very apolitical, you know," he finally said. "It's the only way to survive when you're a seller."

Since El Jeffery had already told me that Elbe was found only when he wanted to be, I decided to just let this pass. Maybe, in Elbe's mind, selling and politics were two totally different things. But I did see his point. "Letting us work here could put you in bad standing?"

"They did ask for the show," El Jeffery pointed out, and neither Elbe nor I needed to ask who "they" were.

"But they asked for it on their home ground," I said.

"All the more reason to have it somewhere else, then."

"Of course. But will they come to somewhere else?"

"And will they think that somewhere else is fair?" asked Elbe.

"We'll talk to Floss and Fred. They know the family rules. It's their house, after all." I was almost out the door when I thought to ask, "Can you wait here? Or, better, will you?"

Elbe shuffled a bit behind his counter, then nodded. But it was easy to see he was reluctant.

"Five minutes," I promised. "Should El Jeffery stay as collateral?"

"I'm certainly worth it," said the griffin, "but I'll stay for a chance to chat with my cousin instead."

I stopped half out the door clutching my package.

"Is 'cousin' figurative or literal?"

"Oh, literal," Elbe said. "You've just never seen my feet."

I found Tonio, Lucia, and Max dipping tortilla chips in pale green salsa, and I realized just how hungry I was. Lucia's sock puppet lay on the table, flattened, eyes staring at nothing, boa draped like a small resting snake. I grabbed a handful of chips and dropped my package on the table. "For Floss," I explained, and then I told them my idea for staging at Elbe's.

"I like it," Tonio said when I was finished. "Neutral space."

"I haven't seen it," Max said. "You really think it'll work for a stage?"

"Probably a whole lot better than anything Floss's family will supply," I said through my mouthful of chips. "But you can see for yourself. Elbe swore he'd wait five minutes."

Tonio launched himself out of his chair. "Let's go, then."

Max and Lucia followed. Lucia's puppet looked

depressed all by itself, there on the table, so I grabbed it and jammed it on my hand as I followed them out the door. The puppet's taffeta skirt rustled.

Elbe's Emporium was shifting just a bit as we got there, like it was ready to move on and was being held in place by a leash. Tonio, who of course had the best eye of all of us for this kind of thing, said, "Perfect. Genius, Persia," before we even got on the porch.

Maybe I'd been wasting my talents all this time, never going space hunting. Maybe my eye was better than I thought. I bobbed Lucia's puppet and said, "Thank you," graciously. I guess there's something about having a puppet. You want to use it, make it come to life. Even a sock puppet.

Lucia had already been to Elbe's with Fred so she didn't prowl like Max and Tonio were doing, and she didn't go inside with them. She stood next to me on the porch, under the huge overhang near the prayer flags, and said, "What do you think of Elvira?" and pointed to the puppet on my hand.

"Oh, the heroine!" I said. "Comfy. What is she? Wool?"

She nodded. "It wicks sweat. Floss and I thought several of them might make a chorus—one person could work two at a time, and they'd sort of match the star."

I gave Elvira back to her. "Makes sense. And they're easy to make sing."

"Sing, sing, sing," Lucia corrected. "But I'm still worried about that stage. A nice proscenium with a curtain would make everything so much more impressive."

"Oh, that's right," I told her. "Floss and I talked. I'll take care of that as soon as we finish up here."

Lucia brightened. "Excellent! Because that looks like now." Max, El Jeffery, and Tonio were back outside, all looking pleased. We walked down the steps in two rows, Lucia and I in front with Elvira, and Tonio, Max, and El Jeffery in back.

"I think Elbe's is perfect," Tonio said. "I'll talk to Floss and Fred and see what we need to do to switch venues."

As soon as all of our feet were on the grass I heard a pop that sounded like a balloon deflating in the distance. When I looked behind me, Elbe's was gone. I turned to El Jeffery. "He'll be back though, right? Tonight? When we need him?"

El Jeffery grinned. "Of course he will. He's Elbe. Now let's go talk to Floss."

As I headed back to Dau Hermanos I heard Lucia, using her Elvira voice, say, "And don't forget that stage opening and those curtains."

XXII

"It does if you pretend hard enough."

*T*onio talked to Floss, and I worked on Lucia's dance hall stage. And since I was working on said stage in Floss's workroom, I listened too. At first Floss was reluctant. She said, "I like the idea of Elbe's, but I hate the idea of changing things at the last minute. They'll think it's a trick and they'll dislike everything we do even more."

Tonio slapped her on the shoulder. "That's the way," he said in a perky cheerleader voice. "Let's keep that positive attitude going."

To make Lucia happy I'd decided to make her stage opening more three-dimensional than one. I was twisting wires together to give the curtains a little swing when Tonio pep-talked Floss, and I almost stabbed myself, I was trying so hard not to laugh. Even though I kept my head down and focused on my curtains, I could feel Floss narrow her eyes at me. But all she said was "Get Fred to ask. They'd never listen to me anyway."

Whatever happened between Tonio and Fred, between Floss and Fred, between Fred and his parents, I never found out. But it was something positive because two hours later Elbe's front porch had become our stage and Elbe had "absolutely, positively" guaranteed that the Emporium wouldn't budge for the duration of the show, for one hour before and for forty-seven minutes after.

"Forty-seven minutes?" I asked Fred.

"Elbe said he wants to help all he can, but he does have a schedule to keep."

"Sure. Of course. And it's a huge favor to go out of his way like this. But forty-seven minutes?"

"He's very precise, is Elbe."

Nicholas looked up from the faerielight he was working with. It was glowing a soft, steady yellow red spotlighty kind of color. "So anything we can't get pulled down gets left behind?"

Fred nodded.

"Right," Nicholas said to us. And to the faerielight he said, "You're the first thing I take with me, then. Because you'd think," he added, talking to us one more time, "once you'd gotten one to work, you'd be on top of the situation, but no. When you get one to cooperate, I think the rest work that much harder to fight against you."

"Depends on the faerielight, I'm beginning to think," Fred said. "It seems that some are more malleable than others."

"Whatever you say. I just know this one and I seem to be getting along quite nicely. For tonight, it's the star."

I gathered up my books of song lyrics and my posters. As I left to get the proscenium opening, I said, "I'm putting everything behind the bar downstairs. An hour isn't anywhere near long enough for a setup, especially since most things will go wrong. It's a dress rehearsal after all. I'm prestaging."

"That sounds reasonable," Fred said. "For all I know about any of this, that is." He began breaking down his faerielight platform. "I'll follow you. And then I need to make sure Max found the candles."

Dau Hermanos was spinning with activity, and none of it had to do with tacos or head cheese. The Outlaws seemed to be everywhere and nowhere at once. Everywhere because I felt like there was always someone on my heels. Nowhere because whenever I needed one particular person they seemed to have just gone the opposite direction.

I ran into Lucia on the stairs, her arms draped in floppy socks, black, gray, and one red, decked out in cancan skirts. She had the stick-puppet chorus line, too, but I was looking for Floss.

I saw Nicholas at the end of the hall headed for the stairs, faerielight cradled in his arms like a baby, but I needed Max.

Tonio moved past me so fast he generated a breeze, but I wanted El Jeffery.

So far, this looked like a typical Outlaw production. The random chaos made me breathe easy, but

I caught a glimpse of Bron and Rohan, eyes wide, as they tried to get out of the multiway traffic that had taken over their place of business.

"It's okay," I assured them as Max and I dropped off several boxes of pillars, tapers, and tea lights. "We're just prepping so that when Elbe comes we can move fast."

"But Persia," Bron protested, "it's pandemonium."

"Yeah. We're getting ready for a show." And I left, dodging El Jeffery and his drum, to find matches because no matter how we'd tried, mortals couldn't seem to light candles any other way.

There'd been minuscule amounts of discussion about whether anyone other than Floss's family and whom-ever they brought with them (and I assumed, of course, that that would be Major) should be allowed to see this thing I insisted on referring to as a dress rehearsal. Minuscule because Floss had said, in a flat no-argument voice, "No," and Fred, when asked, said, "Floss is right. Don't bring in anyone else."

"But if we have outsiders, we'll have more help in

audience participation," I'd said. "I'm pretty sure you were right when you said your family won't play."

"Like I said before, we'll do the participation ourselves if we have to," Floss had responded.

Fred's elbows had been on the table when he pointed one long index finger in agreement. "We can't ask anyone else because Mother won't let them in. Father will go along with her just because he usually does." Fred stopped and took in an audible breath. "She's a strong personality, is mother."

Floss had snorted. "To say the least."

"Exactly." Fred had raised both shoulders, then dropped them. "Feron is anyone's guess, but if he's there I'm sure it's safe to say that he won't be on our side. My suggestion is to pretend that Bron and Rohan are part of all this and let them be the audience plants."

"So this is all more dangerous than I'm pretending it is?" I'd asked.

"Are you pretending?" Fred had sounded interested.

I'd looked around the dinner table, looked at all

my friends, and said, "Of course I'm pretending. I'd never get anywhere otherwise."

Floss had nodded. "You're absolutely right. Just don't forget which part is true and which is the game."

"If games are supposed to be fun I'm not sure this qualifies," Tonio had said.

"It does if you pretend hard enough," Lucia had replied. "And remember, that's what we're good at."

"So, no other audience," I'd said, just to clarify.

"Right," various voices had assured me.

So, while we'd generally discussed this, and made a decision, in the end it didn't matter one bit. When Elbe and his rainbow-bedecked Emporium appeared in the field next to Dau Hermanos there were at least thirty assorted beings gathered on the porch. I saw two who looked like they were related to Reginald, a tall, tall thin woman dressed in sheer blue, a tiny brown person in a pink sprigged dress and Wellington boots, and an identical trio with purple hair, nose rings, and pointed ears. And that was just my first look.

On my second look I saw, off to my left, what must have been some of Lucia's eye-corner creatures. I couldn't quite get a read on them, but an aura of danger dangled in that direction. Every time I tried to face them head-on, they disappeared.

While I was trying to catch a glimpse of the eye-corner creatures Fred said, "Elbe brought an audience."

"Yeah," I said. I was still trying to turn the flickers in my eyes into something substantial. "And maybe more than we can see right now." I looked past my shoulder again and caught an outline, nothing more. "Are those things dangerous?" I asked.

Fred said, "What things?"

Floss, coming up behind me with her arms full of Edgar, stopped and stared hard at Elbe's porch. "I thought we said no company," she growled.

"I certainly didn't invite them," Fred said.

"And Elbe said he wasn't political," I said, "so it couldn't have been him." I'd given up on finding what I couldn't see. There wasn't enough time to chase illusions. Instead I tried to keep my lyric lists and posters from tumbling into a pile of talus on Elbe's front lawn.

El Jeffery stopped trundling his unicycle. He had a marching band snare hung around his neck. "Elbe not political?" He laughed. "Of course he's political. He plays all sides against one another every day. He just pretends that he doesn't."

I widened my eyes at the griffin. "You were there, earlier today. You heard him say he's apolitical. You even asked how he'd get himself into trouble if he helped us."

El Jeffery shrugged. "Two different issues, I think."

"No, they're not," I muttered.

"None of that matters now," Tonio said. "They're here. We're here. Let's move them so we can get to work."

A voice behind us said, "This should be fun, shouldn't it? It's so nice to have everyone together again, too. Like Homecoming. Plus."

The voice was weaker than it had been the last time I'd heard it, but the poking, prodding nastiness made it easy to recognize. Major.

Tonio didn't stop walking, didn't stop balancing

his boxes of candles. Floss didn't turn, just kept going toward Elbe's, holding Edgar. Lucia, Nicholas, Fred, and El Jeffery moved forward, although I noticed Nicholas's armload of faerielight shiver and shift. But I stayed where I was, rooted in the moment. So I was the one who heard Max say, "I do so hope it was the rough crossing that put you in the shape you're in. You look like hell." He examined Major critically, then added, "But damn it, you look so much better than I'd hoped."

That, coming from Max, who was usually so gentle, shocked me. I turned a full 180 degrees. Max stood like he would have if he'd been in a boxing ring. He looked ready to start sparring, looked like he would have already smashed a fist into Major if he hadn't been carrying my stage. The little red and gold curtains quivered on their wires. Somehow, with that puppet in his hand, he looked more dangerous than I'd ever seen him.

Major looked close to dreadful. He was pale, his hair was long and uneven, and there was stubble on his cheeks. His clothes looked like the same ones he'd been wearing when we'd left the chocolate factory that last late night, and they looked like they'd seen a lot of wear since then. There were deep rings under his eyes, the kind that came with weariness and pain, and one arm was in a sling. When he moved he moved stiffly, using the kind of moves people make when everything hurts. His eyes traveled up and down Max and he said, "You look absolutely adorable with your little puppet stage."

The fingers on Max's free hand clenched. I stepped in front of him and said, "Actually, it's my little puppet stage. I just didn't have a carrying hand. Max, could you make sure that Lucia knows it's here? She was worried about it."

He breathed deep enough that I could see his chest rise, nodded, and left.

Major said, "Ah. Defending him. How sweet."

"Actually, I thought I was defending you. You look like you could be blown away by a light breeze, and Max is ever so much more than that." I shrugged. "But, if I think about it more, maybe you're right. Max would probably just kill you, and that might look a tiny bit bad for him. Even here."

Reginald came up and stood close to Major. His own protection. In his irritating rumble he said, "I can take care of her for you."

Before all of the words were out of Reginald's mouth, an older version of Fred materialized. "Materialized" because at the beginning of the sentence he wasn't there and at the end of it he was. Simple as that. It was like watching a magician at work. The newcomer was as blond as Floss, and taller and heavier than Fred in a way that suggested brute strength. He had an air of entitlement to him too, as if he were the kind of person who was used to getting just what he wanted without having to work for it.

"Now, Reginald," he chided. "Remember, we're only here as observers. You, me, and my good friend Major." He raised his voice on the last three words, which had to make them carry to Elbe's porch, had to make them float right over to Fred and Floss.

I saw Floss stiffen, but she didn't turn around. I saw Fred's hands hesitate as he helped Nicholas with the faerielight platform, but he recovered and straightened a piling. And I knew, without a doubt, that I was meeting Feron for the first time.

I looked at Reginald; I looked at Major. Then I looked at Feron. Similarities between them were plain, but it was obvious who was in charge here, and it wasn't Major. Feron smiled at me, a dragon smile. "I'll leave you to get reacquainted," he said, and he walked away from us, headed to a grove of trees a small distance away from Elbe's.

I looked one more time at Major and, for a flash of a second, I wondered what we'd all been so scared of for so long. With Feron there, it was as if I'd seen Major for the first time as exactly what he was— someone with a modicum of power who had dreams of grandeur. But it was only for that second. As soon as Feron was seven long, graceful strides away, Major was in charge again. Maybe Major was all an illusion, but if he was, he was a particularly well-imagined one. He still made me feel ripples on my skin, as if someone was scratching a blackboard.

"I can take care of her," Reginald growled again, and this time he sounded hopeful.

But Major shook his head and never looked at the troll. "I'm fine. Go with Feron."

Reginald shrugged, a movement like a large stone being tumbled by a very fast-moving stream, turned on his heel, and left.

"Why are you here?" I asked suddenly, and I really wanted to know. "You've been after us all this time. I know Tonio's great, but really, give it up."

Major chuckled, but there wasn't any humor there. He said absolutely nothing, just watched me for what felt like hours, then shrugged. "I can tell you because there's not a thing you can do to stop it. Not now. Tonio's the least of it."

"Yeah. Right," I said.

"No. You obviously don't understand. It's all about me. It always has been. Tonio was the add-on. The frosting on the cake, so to speak, but with what's available to me now, he's nothing. I followed you here, yes, but by the time I did that, you were all practically incidental. I must admit, after multiple trips with Feron, I thought it'd be easier to get through on my own. That was my biggest miscalculation because, as you can see, I met up with some damage. But I made it. And Feron and I are working together again, just like we did in our world, making sure there are drinks and dust enough for anyone who wants them."

"That was you? All the pink and purple drinks at home? That was you?"

He laughed, and he got the humor just right. I thought for a brief second of how good an actor he could have been if he'd channeled his energy in a different direction. "Who else? It was for old times' sake that I dropped the blame on Tonio. In fact, old times are why I convinced Feron to have you put on your little show, with its obvious outcome. All of us together, one more time. It's really a shame I don't have a paper to write for here, isn't it?"

"So no matter what you say, it really is us you're after."

He waved his arm, the one that wasn't in the sling, in the air, the universal gesture of a blow off. "At this point what happens to your little group doesn't matter to me in the least. Although it will make Feron very happy to have his meddling sister and probably his brother, too, gone from here for good. Then the place can be ruled the way it should be, without the worry of interference. And I must admit that seeing all of you taken down will be pure pleasure for me."

I thought of all the lives he'd been wrecking, both here and at home, and I shook my head in frustration.

He beamed at me. "When I got here I courted Feron's damnable family. I courted that bastard troll. And it worked. I'm getting exactly what I want, exactly what I need, because they all love me now."

I thought of what I'd just seen of Feron. I doubted that he loved anyone but himself.

Major was still talking. "After you lose this idiotic charade—and you will lose, believe me—then I'll be free to get on with my life. I'll have my own little corner of Faerie to do with just as I please. It's been promised. I'll have a staging spot, one where I can go back and forth between worlds, one where I can gather dust and drinks for transport."

"That to and fro didn't work too well for you last time, did it? Your travel arrangements must have been botched," I said. I sounded braver than I felt.

"Don't worry your pretty little head."

I winced at both his assumption and his choice of the words "pretty little head."

Major kept talking. "I've got it all straightened out now. It's perfect. A hideout, a money source, and hell if I won't be set for life! Then absolutely anything can happen."

With an almost audible click I understood exactly what he was talking about. I felt like I was scrying through a crystal. He thought he could pull off a Faerie coup. I laughed out loud. The Feron I'd seen and the Feron Major knew would have had to be dark and light twins for something like that to happen. "Don't be ridiculous! Feron and his family would never let you do anything to touch their authority." I didn't know Floss's family, but this was something I was sure of.

"Think what you want. I tell you, Feron's already promised. And if he's promised, it's as good as done. The royal family is getting old, you know." He let that statement hang in delicate balance on the air before he added, "The troll and I will share at the start, on that little piece of land that he owns. It won't be hard, though, to keep a troll busy." He stopped and smiled. "He'd be fabulous let loose at home with a pocketful of dust, wouldn't he?"

The thought of Reginald, with his high menace and low intelligence, set loose in my town with pixie dust, was enough to make me queasy.

Still smiling, Major added, "He's so easy to manage. And he's so damned primal he won't know I've taken over until it's too late to do anything about it. And you know how it goes. Once you've got a toe-hold . . ."

He was so pleased with himself. "I could tell them what you're planning," I said.

"Feel free. Tell anyone you'd like. They'd never believe you. Not a friend of Floss's."

He half turned away from me, then stopped, flashed a tooth-baring grin, and said, "Have a great show."

There wasn't one thing to say to that, so I just watched him go. And as I watched I saw what could only be the arrival of Fred and Floss's family.

The woman had hair that matched Floss's dandelion fluff, but it was cotton white instead of yellow. The man was as tall as Fred and walked with his easy confidence. They were followed by a small entourage, including standard bearers who were making their banners flap in a stiff breeze that no one else seemed to feel. I saw Major walk over to Feron, saw them meet the royal family, saw them chatting like old friends. I fast-walked up to Elbe's porch.

Fred and Floss knew the rest of their family was there. I could tell by the set of their shoulders and what seemed to be an absolute aversion to turn and put Elbe's front door behind them. But they didn't say anything, just began to shoo beings off the porch and onto the grass.

When the little woman with the Wellingtons passed me I could see that she held a placard on a pole. It was small because she was small, but I could still read it. *Puppets 10, Rulers 0.* Floss read it too. She had to have, because what else was there about this situation that could make her lips curve in a half-hearted grin?

Tonio motioned all of us to come inside of Elbe's. "We're down to forty-three minutes, people." He looked at each of us, really looked. "We need to work like hell, but we can do this."

As a pep talk it left something to be desired, but its message was clear. But before everyone could leave to follow Tonio's instructions, I said, "I just talked to Major."

Movement ceased, and many pairs of eyes focused hard on me.

"And?" Tonio finally asked.

"And apparently we're no longer what he's after. We never really were. The whole thing at home was more stick-it-to-Tonio than anything else. Because once he met Feron, he convinced himself that we were nothing compared with getting his own little corner of Faerie to play with."

Floss shrugged dismissively and said, "No problem, then. They'd never agree to that."

"Even with Feron on his side?" I asked. "Because I know you heard your brother's voice out there. He's counting on ousting both you and Fred, by the way.

Then I guess he'd be the only heir."

Floss huffed out a breath that sounded violent. She glared at all of us with fierce, bright eyes. "Damn him," she said in a very gentle tone that scared me more than a screaming fit would have. But she seemed positive enough when she said, "But even with Feron on his side, it won't happen. This is my parents' life, Persia. They're not going to give even a smidgen of it away. And if, by some unheard of chance they ever decided they didn't want something, they'd certainly never give it to a mortal."

"Apparently they already have," I said. "Major says it's all set. As soon as we lose—and he's willing to guarantee that, practically—he gets to share rule of Reginald's land. Major's convinced that pretty soon it'll be all his, what with Reginald not being the brightest being inside of Faerie. Major's talking about sending him to our world with a pocketful of pixie dust. In fact, Major, with Feron's help, is the source for the drinks and dust that were bouncing all over the place just before we left."

"Huh," Tonio said in a speculative voice. "Is that

right?" He breathed in and out, then added, almost to himself, "I thought he was too lazy, so why doesn't that surprise me?"

"Because he's a nasty little bastard?" Nicholas asked.

I glanced at him and raised my eyebrows, but Nicholas just shrugged one shoulder.

Tonio said, "Probably just because of that."

I said, "Well, yeah, of course because of that. But think about it—why would Major lie, especially to me? I'm not important enough to lie to. And he's so proud of himself he practically glows. After he gets rid of Reginald, Major says he can go anywhere."

Fred shook his head, a hard, positive motion. "It won't work. First, he'd have to keep getting Feron to supply him with drinks and such. If he's hoping to make a profit on that, he can kiss it good-bye. Feron isn't the type to give anything away, least of all money. He'll never deal. Second, even if Major manages to hold that little piece of land, he'll never get more. Third, Floss is right. Our parents aren't going to give out one single thing. Nothing," he added in a

312

flat voice, "to anyone, including Feron."

"Still if he's working with Feron . . . ," Tonio muttered. "The two of them do seem to be adept at wreaking havoc." Then he visibly shook himself. "But we have a show to put on, people. If we don't do that, at least, they've already won and we won't have even made an attempt to stop any of this. We won't be here to try to do anything. So I repeat, work like hell." He glanced at each of us in turn, nodded as if some unasked question had been answered, then said, "And make it fucking great." And he was gone.

"He's right, you know," Floss said, and she was very calm. "There is no way we let them win without a fight. Let it go. We're not in any worse shape than we were before."

Max said, "Right. Now move, people!"

We followed Max's direction to the letter. Everyone was everywhere at once, it seemed. The worst part was setting the stage. Doing that with an audience watching was off-putting. First, we could feel the eyes on us all the time. Second, we could hear the comments, like a backdrop to every move we made.

Statements like, "Doesn't look like much, does it?" and "They can't be done yet, can they?" are not confidence-producing. The best we could do was try to pretend that there was no one there at all, and that we were all cheery and bright. Sometimes acting came in handy for the most interesting things.

Fred and Nicholas had decided to let their faerie-light be stationary. They said they were worried that a bike ride might "upset" it. Now they put it on its stand just as the shadows started to stretch across the grassy space in front of Elbe's.

A phalanx of fireflies surrounded Fred. First he looked surprised; then he looked like he was listening. Finally I saw him smile. "You certainly aren't required, but you'd be most welcome," he said. The fireflies settled in the corners of Elbe's porch and began to blink soft light into the dark spaces.

I nudged Tonio, who was wrestling the dance-hall scrim. He looked up, blinked twice, and nodded. "We won't need half of those candles, after all," he said.

Max carried stools out, three of them, for sock

puppet workers and backup singers, and started lighting the candles we would need.

El Jeffery paced both the porch and the grass at the base of the steps. He wheeled his unicycle through both areas as well, and finally left it on its side in the grass. It looked like a sleeping giraffe. "More room," he explained, in case one of us was watching or listening.

But really, none of us were. I hung posters over the railing using candles in little ceramic bowls as both weights and illumination. I put my lyric lists on top of the stair post. When Floss called me I went into Elbe's and found her sorting sock puppets. Edgar leaned by the door, ready to be brought to life by Lucia, and the chorus line of rod puppets stood stiff and straight in their green ballet skirts.

"Put these outside, please," Floss said, waving at her stack of socks. "Two on each chair. Then find out where in the world Lucia went."

I frowned. "What do you mean? She brought the socks in. She brought the chorus line in. I saw her."

Floss shook her head, impatience evident in the

movement. "She brought them in, yes, but she said she needed accessories and left again."

"But we've only got . . ." I tried to find a clock, but all of the ones in Elbe's seemed to be operating in different time zones.

"Twenty-eight minutes," Floss muttered. "And I know. But she insisted she needed two bouquets and a minitambourine and that we'd be glad we had them."

I shook my head, but I didn't say anything. I just gathered the socks and arranged them on the three stools, the middle one with Elvira because, since she was Mr. Fox's main adversary, I thought it was important that she be in the center. That was one reason. The other was that I liked her and I thought she deserved it. On the right stool I placed one blue and one charcoal sock; on the left, one dark blue and one blood red.

"And where you came from I don't know," I said to the red puppet as I put it down.

Max heard me and glanced at the sock puppets "The red one?" he asked. "That one's mine. I'm now half socked in the service of art."

I managed a weak grin. "We can call her Maxine then, just for you." He chuckled, low in his throat.

"Twenty minutes," Tonio said, and I went back inside to see if there was something else Floss needed done. She handed me the chorus line and said, "Whoever pulls the curtains on the stage gets them, too."

XXIII

"Points lost, I'd say."

The faerielight was glowing red orange on its stand. The corners of the porch were a soft, firefly gold. There was just enough of a breeze that the leaves whispered poetry through the tree grove where Floss's family had set up camp. Major and Feron, chummy as friends who shared a locker, were with them. The sky was the pure blue that comes before twilight, and the moon was curled on its back, toes pointed north.

Edgar was onstage, the sock puppets were as ready as sock puppets could be, and El Jeffery was pacing, his drum bumping against his side. The puppet stage curtain was drawn. The chorus line was toward the back of the porch, stiff and, for the time being, lifeless. Tonio and Max were straightening the dance-hall scrim. Floss was doing something magical with honky-tonk piano noises, and Fred and Nicholas were standing on the grass, checking the stage for dark edges.

Lucia still wasn't back. I kept looking for her, kept listening for the jingle of that little tambourine, but there was nothing. I was going to find Tonio—talk to him about the fact that we had no Lucia and where was she when we needed her so badly, but first I had to hand out the lyric lists.

I never got my chance to talk to Tonio because, just as I handed out my last booklet of lyrics, there was Bron, striding toward us with steps so long he might have been wearing seven-league boots. As he came close, I said, "Don't worry, you won't miss it." I decided he was almost as good to ask as Tonio since he was coming from the direction Lucia had gone, so I added, "And you haven't seen Lucia, have you?" Then I saw his face.

"Persia." He stopped hard and fast, like he'd run

into an immovable force. Like he'd run into Reginald. "Here. Before I lose every shred of control that I have." He thrust a crumbled sheet of paper at me, and I stood there and held it between my thumb and first finger. I had that breathless feeling that comes when you know, even before you're sure, that the news is going to be bad, and I'd already had way too much bad news for one night. I felt the way Nicholas must have felt on that day so long ago, the day when Tonio had had him read the subpoena. If I didn't read it, we could stay balanced on the knife edge of knowing and not knowing forever. That would be the safe thing to do.

Bron apparently did not share my desire to stay balanced. "Do you just want me to tell you?" he asked, and the stretch and strain in his voice meant that he already had, really. He didn't wait for an answer. "Reginald has Lucia."

"What?" The syllable came out like a stage whisper, my shock putting such a hard snap on the "t" that all the Outlaws heard, stopped what they were doing, and stared at me. I barely noticed.

"What do you mean? Lucia went to get bouquets

and a tambourine. I asked, just a little bit ago. Floss promised she'd be right back." I wanted to make Bron say he was wrong. To make my case stronger, I pointed and said, "And Reginald's right there, with Major and Feron." I pointed toward the group under the trees, which was when I noticed the absolute absence of the troll.

By now we had two minutes to showtime, and instead of us taking our places, breathing deep, and running our own personal mantras, we were gathered in a knot around Bron. I still held the note much as I would have held a dead rat's tail.

"Reginald has Lucia," I repeated Bron's words.

"And he says," Bron stopped to pry the note from my fingers, "I want to get this exact. 'Win and she comes back. Leave and she stays with me.'" He read more, this time to himself. "Right. Yes. The terms—"

Major interrupted him. He'd come up so quietly I hadn't heard him at all. "Not starting on time? Points lost, I'd say. And you really can't afford to lose all that many points when you're starting out with a deficit like this." He pointed toward our stage with scorn.

Floss took two slow, gentle steps toward Major. "Where is she?" Her tone was Saturday afternoon relaxed, but I saw him shift back before he stopped himself. "Lucia was not in the terms of the agreement," Floss added.

"Things change. You know that. Everything is always in flux."

Floss didn't bother to answer. She brushed past him the way she'd pass by an uninteresting display at Elbe's and walked with flat steps to the little cluster around her parents.

"Floss, dear, how lovely to see you." Her mother's voice was clear and carried beautifully in the soft evening air, and I suddenly hated her. "We're all so pleased you've decided to come back home. Your brother has especially been missing you."

"If you mean Fred, we've talked. If you mean Feron, I doubt it."

"Why, Floss, whatever do you mean?" Feron asked.

Floss stiffened, but she was royalty, after all, and it showed now. She didn't look at Feron, didn't speak to him. Instead she directed both looks and words toward her mother. "Actually, Mother, as you know, I've been at home for quite some time now. I just didn't bother to stop at your house." Her voice carried to the crowd even better than her mother's had. "I came over here to mention that if anything happens to Lucia that doesn't involve all of us, I will personally guarantee bad times in your future."

"Threats?" said her mother. "From you?"

"Promises," Floss snarled.

"I suppose banishment is preferable as a group activity." Her mother said this in about the same voice that she might have used to read the weather report from the morning paper.

"I repeat, whatever happens, Lucia had better be a part of it."

Floss's mother waved her hand, royalty to her subject. "I have nothing to do with your missing person. When this is all over perhaps you can discuss your problems with Major or Feron. Major is so charming, and of course, you know your brother." And she very deliberately turned her back on her daughter.

Floss spoke to that back, saying, "You might want

to watch the company you keep. Some people from both inside and outside of Faerie are Janus-faced. You never know who they might be allies with."

Her mother made no response.

Tonio spoke then, from near Elbe's porch, from a spot close to Bron and me. His voice was conversational and easy, and it was obvious that he was directing his comments to Major. "Lucia's my friend. Lucia's got nothing to do with you and me, or your little dreams of glory, or whatever the hell you and your friend have up your sleeves. Get her back here. Because however this plays out, if she's not here when we're through, you'll be very, very sorry."

Major smiled. "It's interesting when the stakes change, isn't it?"

I went and stood next to Tonio. Max moved to his other side. Nicholas, Fred, and El Jeffery stood in a solid row behind us. Tonio returned Major's smile, but his was sharp-edged and glittery. "Just remember what I said. Because I can make promises just as nicely as Floss."

Floss was back with us by then, standing next to

me. The crowd on the grass was barely breathing. I knew they were waiting to see what would happen next. The air was so thick with tension I felt my lungs fill with the stuff. I coughed and said, "Don't you all think it's past time for this show to start?"

I pressed Floss's hand and turned to start the long walk to Elbe's. She followed me and, like a parade, one by one, everyone else fell into line behind us.

We had to change things. Floss, not Lucia, worked Edgar, and he was feisty and strong, scary and rude. In spite of my worry about Lucia I actually had to stifle a snicker when Edgar came out chomping on a big cigar, screaming at the chorus line. I thought that all the screaming was probably because that was how Floss herself felt at this point. Aside from worries about Lucia, Major, her parents, and Feron, she also had to deal with her normal stage worries of puppet magic. Anything else she might have wanted to add, like piano sounds, tapping feet, whatever, was superficial at best.

Fred, not Nicholas or Tonio, helped Max with the extra scrim. When they first tried to set it up, it folded over on itself for one long second. I could see the frustration on both their faces, but then Max gave it a yank and it straightened right up. The yank was vicious, and I wondered if Max was thinking more about Major than about scrims. Max got stuck with the proscenium curtain, too.

Tonio and Nicholas each worked two sock puppets. It seemed that one of them should have been Edgar, and Floss should have been some of the backup singers, but everything was upside down at this point and we were all just doing the best we could do. One of the gray socks never got to move at all, but she wasn't really needed. The cutting anger that Tonio and Nicholas managed to slide into their vocals worked just fine with four puppets instead of five.

I moved the chorus line, but they came downstage instead of up because I had to become Elvira, too. Elvira, when she finally figured out what was happening, wailed her songs like a scar-washed blues singer, voicing all my own pent-up emotions.

And El Jeffery? He beat the hell out of his drum. The beats were staccato slaps, so hard I expected to see his big griffin nails punch right through the drum head. His unicycle lay on the grass like a dead thing, and he gave Floss little boosts of magic whenever he could.

Elbe abandoned his apolitical stance and worked too, charting the fireflies' tracks to keep as much light on us as possible. He even came up with the idea of sending batches of them out into the crowd. They were like little night-lights that the throng used to help them read the lyrics. And he definitely got the audience participation started, singing out "Five foot two, eyes of blue" when Elvira made her first appearance. Elbe had a lovely tenor voice.

Was it the best Outlaw performance ever? Not by any unit of measurement known to humans or fey. By the time we were done, though, Edgar had lost his production company, Elvira had exposed him for the cad that he was, and, most important, she was still alive. She'd also regained the honor of his previous stars.

Then someone in the audience called out, "Come on home now, all is forgiven." Everyone seemed to recognize that lyric, and we joined together in a rousing chorus of the music hall favorite "That's What

You Think." It was a fitting end to Elvira's story. I breathed out, long and slow, and I felt that we'd done something we could be proud of.

We bowed; the audience applauded and laughed. Edgar and Elvira bowed too, and the applause got even louder. Then I saw Major, Feron, and Floss's parents walking out of their little grove of trees. They were walking away from us, rejection apparent in every line of their bodies.

The voice that yelled, "Wait!" belonged to Elbe. Thank goodness for Elbe. I think we were all too stunned to say or do anything. We'd been given no answer and we had no Lucia. Were we all just supposed to stand there, emotionally spent, exhausted, and hoarse-voiced, the sweat drying on our skins in the cool evening air?

Floss's mother turned. "Yes?" she said, and her voice was quite a few degrees below the outside air temperature.

Major turned with her. "You have your answer, I think," he said. "We're leaving. And really, Tonio. You thought this little charade would win us over?

Please." His laugh was nicely done. Just enough vitriol to be insulting.

But Tonio was thinking. Tonio was fast on his feet. "Let them decide," he said, pointing to the crowd on the grass.

"Impartial judges." Elbe was approving.

"Applause?" Nicholas asked.

But I remembered the little woman in the Wellingtons and the sprigged dress. I remembered her sign, "Puppets 10, Rulers 0."

"No," I said. "Match points." I ran up Elbe's stairs. "Wait," I yelled as I went inside.

Elbe followed me so I was out in under a minute, pads of paper and boxes of pomegranate- and apricot-scented markers in my arms. "Rate it," I called to the crowd. "Rate the show. Ten out of ten is perfect. Zero out of ten is the worst."

"Don't give them ideas," Nicholas whispered into my ear. His breath was warm where it brushed against my cheek. I almost grabbed for him, just to feel the warmth and life of him, but I handed out pads of paper instead. By the time I'd reached the back of the crowd, marveling one more time at the diversity of the inhabitants of Faerie, those in the front were waving their papers. In spite of everything, I'd enjoyed seeing these people, performing for them. If I really could see inside, all I saw here were decent beings trying to survive and be happy. I turned around and saw my friends watching the crowd. Floss and Fred were standing together, eyes bright. El Jeffery stood at Floss's right side, and I say again if a griffin could smile, that's what he was doing. Tonio and Max were holding hands. And next to me Nicholas called to the royal family, "Come up to Elbe's porch. See what the audience thinks."

When the chill voice of Floss's mother swept over us, I was almost surprised that she was still there. Almost. I didn't want to even try to look inside her. I didn't need to. I knew from the outside that she was the kind of person who'd believe she'd won, no matter what.

I'd always thought cold air dropped, but her personal patch of cold air, her voice, was streamlined as a dirigible. It arrowed straight toward Floss and Fred.

"I hardly think we need to worry about what *they* say."

I could see the derisive quotes around the word "they," clear and clean as if they were painted in the evening sky. There was a stunned silence, then a mounting rumble from the crowd behind Nicholas and me. It sounded mutinous. Then another voice floated over it, calm and filled with a sadness that made my heart ache.

"Then why did you stay?" Floss asked. "Even for those few minutes? Because that's always your answer, isn't it? Ignore the ones who are affected. Live in your insular, little world. Don't make any effort to talk to real people. You knew what your answer would be even before you floated that note to us two days ago."

The royal family turned their backs as if they'd rehearsed it. As a brush-off it was very effective. Even in the deepening twilight, even without extra firefly light, I could see that there was some kind of discussion going on. Major raised his arm, pointed back at all of us, and laughed. His teeth flashed white in the gloom. Next to him Feron looked thick, relaxed, and substantial.

Then Fred said, "You finally have a chance to do something right," and his voice was childlike, gentle. He paused. No one moved. "I know you have it in you," he added after what felt like a decade-long wait.

Major huffed out a smiling breath that I could almost feel. Reginald had reappeared, and I thought that he must have done so by magic. Maybe he was better at that stuff than Fred and Bron thought. He moved to stand between Feron and Major.

Then slowly, like he was one of our puppets being dragged by his strings, Fred and Floss's father turned and began to walk back to us, back to the crowd. His wife grabbed at him, but he shook his head. Major, no longer smiling, caught at his sleeve, but the duke jerked away. Feron stepped in front of his father and the man sidestepped him with the precision of a football player taking the ball to the end zone.

He walked between me and Nicholas as if we weren't taking up ground. He walked through the crowd as if they weren't there. Major followed at a fast clip, and watching him was like watching a little dog chasing after a big dog. Even with the puppet-walk of the duke, it looked like Major was marching in double time. I looked toward Feron and saw his hands twisting into fists.

Everything that had happened since we'd left home came together and made me want to choke out a nervous laugh. Or maybe that was the tension. I caught my tongue gently between my teeth and didn't make a sound. The night had grown so dense and stretched that it felt like the air itself was screaming.

When Fred and Floss's father reached the steps of Elbe's porch he looked up at his son and daughter for what felt like a very long time. Now the night wasn't screaming. It was holding its breath, waiting for something to be put right, something that had been running wrong for a very long time.

"I believe you have a rating method of some type set up for this . . ." He paused, cocked his head, and said, ". . . performance?"

Floss looked long and hard at her father. Then she nodded. "I believe we do. Turn around and see what the audience thinks." She repeated the line Nicholas had said to Major, but this time someone did what they were supposed to do.

Fred and Floss's father looked at his children standing on Elbe's porch and then, still using those measured puppet moves, turned his back to the Emporium. Elbe, who was tucked half out of sight in his doorway, did something complicated with his hands that ended in a finger snap. Fireflies swarmed over the crowd. They illuminated the papers, papers held stiff between hands of all shapes, sizes, and colors. The air smelled strongly of the markers I'd handed out—apricot and pomegranate.

Major stood next to the duke, facing the Emporium instead of the crowd. I could tell that his eyes were boring straight into Tonio just by the set of his head and shoulders. Behind me, I could feel Feron's eyes locked tightly on our group of Outlaws, and it took all my self-control to keep looking straight ahead, to pretend that he wasn't there. I was close enough to the scene being played out on Elbe's porch that I heard Fred and Floss's father say, in a strangled voice, "Has it been that bad, then?" I saw Major's shoulders slump.

Then Major came back to life and grabbed again for the duke. "Wait! Listen to me," he said through clenched teeth. Without looking at Major, the duke knocked his hand away with a slap of flesh against flesh that must have been heard in the back of the crowd.

At the same time Fred, still using his gentle voice, said, "They're rating a play. Not your rule, a play." He waited the length of a heartbeat then added, "I do believe, though, that the things said in the play and what's been happening in your rule are very closely aligned. Perhaps they're rating truth."

"I hadn't thought," the duke began in a strangled voice. "I've been so busy . . ."

Floss interrupted to say, "And that's the whole problem right there, isn't it? You didn't think. You don't think. You're never here."

She drew in breath to say more, but Fred dropped a hand on Floss's arm and she blew the breath out in a long, long sigh. Behind me, I heard the rustle of rich fabric against silks and laces.

"Enough," said Fred and Floss's mother. "Leave. We have made our decision. We control this ground and your little parody of a play has done nothing to dissuade me of the worthlessness of your ridiculous way of life. Or of the worth of you remaining in Faerie."

"Ah," said Floss, and it was a flat, one-note word. "But did it make you take a look at the way things are in this particular corner of Faerie?"

"Don't be absurd," their mother snapped. "It's certainly done nothing to make me rethink my rule."

"How strange," Floss said in an even voice, "I never said one word about your rule."

"Your brother did. Voices carry," the duchess said.

Floss shrugged elegantly. The duchess had reached Elbe's steps by then and had reached her husband. "Floss, you never had it in you to make something of yourself. And as for you," she said to Fred, "aligning yourself with your sister may be your tragic flaw. You'd do well to reconsider. Or would you like exile along with this gaggle of misfits?"

"The way things have been going it would be preferable to staying here," Fred said softly.

"Ridiculous. But I should have known. Two worthless, ungrateful children instead of just the one. Thank Mab I have Feron."

Major's head snapped up, like he was imitating Fred's yo-yo. I could hear his choke of laughter. It sounded like a cry of victory.

Floss said, "You raised us, Mother."

"She raised me, too. It's obvious who turned out better," Feron said, pleasure in his voice.

As before, the air around me reacted to something that was on its way. Even before the duke said, "Feron—enough. Martene, control yourself," with a knife edge in his voice, I sensed the night breathing cattails, water lilies, and marigolds. I saw the fireflies shuffle in the breezes.

The duchess whirled on her husband, her hand raised to slap, but he caught her wrist and said in a sharp voice that carried like the buzz of angry bees, "We are a shared rule. Do not force me to change policy and make this a place ruled by only one."

The gasp from the crowd was so hushed that it was almost lost in the fabric rustles as the duchess yanked her hand away and whirled on her heel. Major turned to follow her and was stopped by Feron's hand, heavy on his shoulder. When Feron said, "Your services are no longer required," with crisp precision, it was obvious that Major had suddenly become a hindrance rather than a help.

Major stopped, hard, as if he'd run into a wall, and looked at Feron as if he wasn't sure where to go or what to do. Ignoring the drama behind her, the duchess skirted the crowd as if they were a pond of alligators and disappeared into the edges of darkness.

"Father," Feron began, but the duke said, "Later." Just that one word, but it whipped like a flag in a strong north wind. Feron twisted around and followed his mother.

Major turned in a slow circle. His eyes looked like they were searching for friends. Apparently none were forthcoming. He skittered away following the path Feron and the duchess had taken, and was swallowed by the soft silk of the night.

Three breaths of nothing. Then, stunned, I grabbed at Nicholas. "Did that all mean what I think it meant?"

"I think so," he said, and he grinned like sunshine on a spring day.

"Wow." It seemed inadequate, but I couldn't think of anything else to say.

Nicholas could, though. "Don't you want to see the scores?" He laughed a little, sounding free, and pulled me onto Elbe's porch. We turned and, in fire-fly light we read the papers that were still visible.

"I thought I saw a couple of tens," Nicholas said, wonder in his voice.

"You did," Tonio agreed. "Faerie inhabitants must be very generous."

"Really," Nicholas agreed. "Because we were not tens. We were barely fives."

Tonio stifled a laugh and said, "Always trust your audience."

Bron stood next to Floss, one arm around her in what looked like both protection and support. "I thought it was quite good, myself."

"Not a ten," Floss said to him, and she was fierce. "Wait until you see us really do something."

"You'll stay then?" the duke asked.

Floss tensed again, and Bron called out to the crowd, "Free drinks at Dau Hermanos," which meant rapid dispersal and left only our small group standing on Elbe's porch.

"Thank you," Floss said to him in a tired voice.

Tonio answered for Floss. "We're a family. We'll need to talk things through."

"Part of the family isn't here, though," Max said, a serious edge in his voice, and at the same time I said, "Lucia's still not here. We can't do anything without Lucia."

Why Reginald hadn't left with Major, why he hadn't disappeared again in the slick, stealthy way he'd used when Lucia was taken, I didn't know. Since it was obvious now that it had been Feron, Major, and the duchess all along, tight as Bondo, maybe he'd been excluded from their plans. And there was also the fact that Reginald had proved all along that he clearly wasn't very bright.

Maybe he simply couldn't pick up undercurrents, or, for that matter, overcurrents. Getting Lucia had been his goal. Possibly he'd never even made a plan for what came next. Whatever it was, when every firefly in the area surrounded him Reginald was still there, half turned to stone. As a disappearing trick, it wasn't at all effective. Half stone or not he was still only Reginald.

Fred and El Jeffery got to him first, Fred because of adrenaline anger, I think, and El Jeffery because of his wings. Reginald didn't stand a chance, and he knew it. The fear smell of old blood was strong on him, and as Fred and El Jeffery came close to him, the stone spell dropped away like a boulder crashing into a lake. Reginald stood there alone. He looked naked. From his place near Floss on the porch, Bron said, "He never could get that stone thing. I'm amazed he even tried."

"Desperate times," Tonio murmured.

When Fred told Reginald, "We'll just walk you home," there were glass edges in the sentence that made Max's worst threats sound like a little boy playing grown-up.

After the three of them left, Floss and the duke watched each other, and both looked wary. He must have seen something I didn't catch because he said, "I think I have some things to talk about with your mother," and he faded into the night following his wife's path. He didn't look like a puppet now. He was a man moving with purpose.

Floss collapsed, hard, on Elbe's porch. Bron dropped down next to her and wrapped her in his arms. I heard Floss say, into his shoulder, "Oh, my." It was one of the most un-Floss-like statements ever, but I think it mirrored all our thoughts so well that the rest of us didn't need to say a thing.

Lucia came home, accompanied by a victorious Fred and El Jeffery. "I never even got to draw blood," Fred said, and he sounded vaguely disappointed. Lucia looked stretched around the eyes. A lingering scent of that river water and old blood smell of Reginald clung to her, but she looked strong, alive, aware. I attributed that to Fred, whose chair was so close to Lucia's that they were almost sharing the same seat.

We were in the private room in Dau Hermanos, where we almost couldn't hear the free drinks party at the bar. Tonio and Max were sharing something that was a cross between blackberry wine and cassis. Nicholas and I had a mix of lemonade and beer. Floss, Fred, and Lucia were drinking a straw-colored wine that smelled like windfall apples. El Jeffery was drinking wine too, but his was the color of rubies at midnight. Floss kept grinning at him and squeezing his paws, and even though Lucia was the quietest, all of them, including Fred, were playing some kind of word game that ended each sentence with the line "in a troll's lair." And then Bron brought in a bottle of fizzy, golden hard cider. He was followed by Rohan, who held tiny goblets like flowers between all his fingers.

Once it was poured, Floss picked up a glass of the bright, light-infused wine and said, "We should make a toast."

"We could toast a production that's going to grow in leaps and bounds," Tonio said.

"Mab, let's hope so," said Max, and everyone laughed because he was so very right.

But I had a better idea. "I think we should toast us. We toast the Outlaws. Because that's what we are."

"And always will be," Tonio said, fierce as Floss. "When puppets are outlawed, only outlaws will have puppets!"

"And you've certainly got those," Bron said.

Nicholas laughed and pulled me against him in an embrace so tight I almost spilled my wine. Then there was a crystal-on-crystal clink of glasses, the lights dimmed, and fireflies filled the room.

WHY WE'LL BE STAYING IN FAERIE, AT LEAST FOR THE TIME BEING

Floss and Fred's father now seems to realize that his little corner of the world needs to take another shape.

Without Feron's help, Major's dust and drink delivery service should come to a screeching halt.

Feron's try for a coup should be meeting many more royal questions.

Elbe has promised us a permanent, traveling performance space.

We can do so much puppet magic here!

But mostly? We're staying because we're happy.

ACKNOWLEDGMENTS

Thanks!

Erin Murphy for being the best agent in the world.

Kristin Daly Rens for picking up this project in the middle and being wonderful to work with.

To the people at HarperCollins and Balzer and Bray: Alessandra Balzer and Donna Bray for taking me on, Sara Sargent and Ruta Rimas for assists, Laura Kaplan for publicity, Emilie Ziemer for marketing, Crystal Velasquez and Kathryn Silsand for extraordinary copyediting, and Patty Rosati for school and library coordination.

The Anonymous Writers who let me read bits and pieces to them and critiqued like champions: Emily, Emily, James, Jesse, Jola, and Kat.

Emily Parent for chapter headings, especially "Soggy. Wet Out."

Aileen Finnin for El Jeffery.

Scott Parent for keeping me honest.

Leah Key-Ketter for loving the programs.

Sharon Bryant for encouragement.

Amy Calkins for reading early on.

Barbara Shuman for all those massages.

Guy Shuman for working on the music.

David Shuman just because.

The Andersons, Nelsons, and Musas for always asking.

Nora Lambrecht for liking Floss.

Melissa Lambrecht for good advice.

Melanie Zeck for breakfasts.

Tea Lula for tea and conversation.

Lance Anderson for all those rereads on the train, for not screaming whenever I moaned about the writing, and for just being there.